MISSING HER MORE

KAREN MCQUESTION

PRAISE FOR THE BOOKS OF KAREN McQUESTION

"*Good Man, Dalton* is a sweet confection you'll savor as Midwesterner Greta Hansen arrives in New York City for a job that doesn't exist—and discovers something better than money or fame."

—Christine Nolft, bestselling author of *The Road She Left Behind*

"I was riveted to the page and on occasion brought to tears. A book you don't want to miss."

—Barbara Taylor Sissel, bestselling author of *Faultlines* and *The Truth We Bury* on *Half a Heart*

"Karen McQuestion just keeps getting better! *Hello Love* is an enchanting, impossible-to-put-down novel about big hearts and second chances."

—Claire Cook, *USA Today* bestselling author of *Must Love Dogs*

"An emotional and engaging novel about family . . ."

—Delia Ephron on *A Scattered Life*

"McQuestion writes with a sharp eye and a sure voice, and as a reader, I was willing to go wherever she wanted to take me. After I finished the book, I thought about how I might describe it to a friend, and I settled on . . . 'You should read this. It's good.'"

—Carolyn Parkhurst on *A Scattered Life*

"The plot is fast paced and easy to dive into, making this a quick and exciting read."

—*School Library Journal* on *From a Distant Star*

"I devoured it in one sitting!"

—*New York Times* bestselling author Lesley Kagen on *Edgewood*

"At first glance *Favorite* is a story of a girl and her family learning to cope with loss. But at some point it morphs into a psychological thriller. It's an unexpected but welcome turn that will leave readers on the edge of their seats."

—Jessica Harrison, *Cracking the Cover*

"This story featuring a strong protagonist who has mastered the art of being the new girl will appeal to girls who are fans of this genre."

—*School Library Journal* on *Life on Hold*

"This is an adventure that is sure to appeal to both boys and girls, and I can't wait to read it to my students."

—Stacy Romanjuk, fourth-grade teacher at Hart Ransom School in Modesto, California, on *Secrets of the Magic Ring*

"An imaginative fable about two witches that should excite young readers."

—*Kirkus Reviews* on *Grimm House*

OTHER TITLES BY KAREN MCQUESTION

FOR ADULTS

A Scattered Life

Easily Amused

The Long Way Home

Hello Love

Half a Heart

Good Man, Dalton

Dovetail

FOR YOUNG ADULTS

Favorite

Life on Hold

From a Distant Star

The Edgewood Series

Edgewood (Book One)

Wanderlust (Book Two)

Absolution (Book Three)

Revelation (Book Four)

FOR CHILDREN

Celia and the Fairies

Secrets of the Magic Ring

Grimm House

Prince and Popper

FOR WRITERS

Write That Novel! You Know You Want To . . .

ISBN: 9781688615403

Cover Design by VercoDesign, Unna

❀ Created with Vellum

For the readers who asked for more

CHAPTER 1

*C*ece knew this day would be significant, but she couldn't have anticipated how life-changing it would be, both for her family and for another family, one she hadn't met yet. What she did know was that very soon she'd be facing a battle of the paternal kind. Her father's phone call had made that clear when he said, "Your mother and I will be home this weekend to get things straightened out."

That statement was a sign of a coming storm, she thought. By *get things straightened out*, he meant that he'd be getting *her* straightened out. She'd always been accommodating before, and he expected more of the same this time around. What he didn't know was that she was different now. More decisive, ready to run her own life. The change had been brewing under the surface all along, but she hadn't acted on it until recently, so to him it would certainly seem sudden.

Her new friend, Roger, didn't quite get it. "You're an adult woman with your own company," he said. "Plus, you're wealthy, smart, and beautiful. Why does your dad think he can tell you how to live your life?"

She shrugged. "It's always been that way." Looking at her

family from the outside, it would be impossible to see all the threads that kept them entangled. Pull one thread out and the whole balance was upset, and Cece had definitely done that when she told her father over the phone that she was done with the whole charade he'd set up—her career as a social media celebrity, the business deals set up in her company, Firstborn Daughter Inc., and a nonstop schedule that left her exhausted. There were third graders who had more say in their daily activities.

Looking back, none of it had been her idea. The videos, the fragrance deal, the designer clothing in her name. She'd been talked into things, bit by bit, until she found herself in a life not of her choosing. The worst part was that it was never-ending. Her father was always reaching for more. *Bigger and better* was his motto. Bigger and better. There was no resting, no staying in her comfort zone, just leapfrogging from one thing to the next.

It was exhausting. She was tired of the circus that her life had become. From the outside, she had an enviable life, but the truth of it was that she was miserable to the core.

It had been easy telling him on the phone that she was through with it all. Facing her father in person would be much more difficult. He was strong-willed and would be counting on her to be her usual pliable and sweet self. She knew she'd have to be strong because his weapons of choice were intimidation and a loud voice.

And oh, did she hate when he raised his voice. It cut right through her, making her feel like curling up in defeat.

Still, when her parents came through the front door of their penthouse apartment, they were both smiling, her mother practically glowing despite the long flight from Paris to New York. Both Cece and her eight-year-old sister, Brenna, were waiting in the front room, Cece determined to face her father's wrath head-on, Brenna anticipating the gift that always came after a lengthy trip. Brenna looked at her mother expectantly, noticing

2

that underneath her mother's left arm was a stuffed animal, a toy dog that looked amazingly lifelike. Her mother strode across the room and presented it with a flourish. "For you, my darling. Just as you requested."

Brenna took it from her, a puzzled look on her face. "What I requested?"

Her mother laughed. "Did you forget already? You've been begging for a dog, and here it is. What are you going to name him?"

"But I was talking about a real dog." Brenna's lower lip quivered. "One I could play with and teach tricks."

The air in the room got heavy, and their father frowned. Cece knew that look. He expected both of his daughters to be grateful for all parental efforts, regardless of whether or not they wanted what they were given. He cleared his throat. "Don't be so silly, Brenna. Dogs are a lot of work and completely impractical for city living. The one your mother gave you is every bit as good, and she went to quite a bit of trouble to get it. I think it would be nice if you'd thank her for the thoughtful gift."

Brenna's head dropped. "Thank you for the dog." She glanced up and added, "It's very cute."

Their mother smiled. "You're welcome, Brenna."

"Very good." Their father nodded in approval, order having been restored. "Now why don't you go show Nanny your new gift? We need to talk to your sister."

After Brenna left the room, her father gestured for Cece to sit down. The three of them were positioned in a triangle, she and her mother making the base, her father at the head. A deliberate positioning, she thought.

But Cece had planned a strategy of her own. She knew he could manipulate anything she said, so she'd decided to say little and make each word count.

The conversation went as she knew it would. Her father's

voice was firm and loud, the tone just angry enough to discourage a dissenting viewpoint. He said she was a disappointment. She was ungrateful. He said, "Don't you know how many young women your age would love to have all the opportunities you've been given?" She nodded in an attempt to seem agreeable, but he wasn't waiting for an answer and didn't notice her response. This was a one-man show. Output only. He kept going, shifting from emotional manipulation and heading right to declarative sentences, telling her how it was going to be from now on. "The good news is that I don't think you've done too much damage gallivanting around Central Park after hours. And falling into the pond, of all things. What were you thinking, Cece?" He ran his fingers through his hair and shook his head. "I can make a few phone calls, hire a new PR firm. A lot of celebrities have meltdowns, but lucky for us, Americans love a good comeback story. We can fix this."

Cece kept her face impassive, letting him speak his mind. There was no point in arguing with him.

He wrapped things up by ticking off on his fingers how things would be from now on. Cece guessed that he used the same strategies with his daughters as he used in the boardroom. When he finally finished his tirade, he ended the conversation by saying, "Do you understand?"

Her father, Cece suddenly realized with a shock, was a control freak. All this time she'd thought that he'd been acting in her best interests. She'd believed him when he jokingly called her a beautiful bubblehead, a girl who lacked business sense. Now she saw him for what he was—a man who needed to control everything around him. Well, he wasn't going to control her life anymore.

When a moment went by and she didn't respond, he repeated the question, this time more sternly. "Do you understand, Cecelia?"

This was the point where she was supposed to agree with

him. If she really wanted to get back in his good graces, she'd throw in an apology or two. But that was the old Cece. The new Cece was not going to apologize. She stood up and said, "I understand perfectly, but that's not what is going to happen." She heard her voice begin to quaver, so she took a deep breath before continuing. She could do this. "I've decided that I will be making all the decisions concerning my personal life and First-born Daughter Inc. from now on."

A look of alarm crossed her mother's face, and Cece could almost read her mind. *Let it go, Cece. Just do what he wants to keep the peace.* Her mother was all about keeping the peace, but this was not a time for peace.

Cece just kept talking, reciting the words she'd mentally prepared ahead of time. "I want to thank you for all your help in establishing my career. I am truly grateful, but I'll be going in a different direction at this point."

Her father's face reddened, and she saw his Adam's apple bob as he swallowed the words he really wanted to say. When he did talk, it was clear he was holding himself in check. "I think we should all take a break to think about what's best. We can finish this discussion at dinner."

"That's another thing," Cece said. "I no longer live here, so I won't be at dinner this evening. I still have the same cell phone number, so you can reach me anytime."

Her father's mouth opened, but no words came out. Could it be that he was truly speechless?

Her mother said, "I think we're all tired. We don't need to decide anything definite right this minute. Let's reconnect later and talk when we're less emotional."

Cece nodded. "I'll let the two of you get some rest." She stood up and went over to her mother, giving her a kiss on the cheek. She did the same for her father, who sat statue-like, staring at her as if she'd become possessed. "Goodbye. I'll see you later."

She'd made it almost to the front door when she heard her mother's footsteps behind her. "Cece, wait!"

"Yes?" She turned to face her.

"Where do you live now?" The anguish on her mom's face made her almost regret having moved out of the apartment. It was time, though, and they would have been upset no matter when it had happened.

"Not too far." She smiled. "Greta and I moved into Katrina and Vance's old apartment downstairs."

Her mother leaned in and gave her a hug. She whispered in her ear, "I'll talk to him. Perhaps we can work something out? Maybe if you let him be a consultant or check with him first before you make any big decisions? He really does know best about such things."

Cece shook her head. "I know you mean well, Mom, but I need to do this on my own."

CHAPTER 2

When Brenna had left the room, she hadn't gone to show Nanny her new toy as instructed. It wasn't even possible since Nanny had already left for day. Normally she'd be there, but when Cece came by at lunchtime she told Nanny she was free to go home, that she would stay with her sister until their parents arrived. Brenna waited around the corner in the next room, wanting to see what would happen to her sister. Change made her nervous, and now everything was changing. Vance and Katrina—her sister's friends, who used to be around nearly every day—had up and moved away. Brenna had just gotten used to their cousin, Greta, who'd moved in with them for the summer, and then Greta had moved out, taking Cece with her.

Everyone was leaving her.

"I'm just downstairs, silly," Cece had said. "You don't even have to leave the building to come and see me." Brenna knew she was right, but it didn't matter. Cece's room was now shockingly empty, and Brenna felt adrift. When Nanny wasn't there, Cece was her source of comfort. Who would she go to when she had a bad dream? Who would reassure her during thunderstorms? She certainly wasn't going to take the elevator down-stairs for such things. It felt like Cece was so far away.

As she listened to her father venting at her sister, a knot twisted in her tummy. He was keeping his voice level, but still he was loud. He was always loud, even when he wasn't upset. Sometimes when she and her mother visited him at his office, she could hear his voice from down the hall. The words perme-ated the walls and sliced through doors. His voice was a force of nature, like the wind, a sound that threatened to knock you over. Brenna tried to stay on his good side so she wouldn't have to hear that voice aimed right at her.

She clutched the toy dog to her front for comfort. The dog was cute, as plush animals went, and probably something she'd have loved in her younger days, maybe when she was a little kid of four or five. As it was now, a toy was no substitute for the real thing. She wanted a dog who would greet her at the door, happy to see her. She'd imagined a dog nuzzling her with his nose, the equivalent of a kiss. One who would curl up next to her in bed, keeping her company when she felt alone. This dog was only synthetic fur and stuffing. A poor substitute for the real thing.

Brenna kept her ears open, listening as her father wound down from a very long speech. When he asked Cece if she understood for the second time, Brenna sucked in her breath, waiting. Brenna was certain that Cece knew the right thing to say, but she didn't say it. Instead she came back, telling her father she would be running things her way. Brenna waited for the explosion that was sure to come, but Cece held the floor, telling them she wouldn't be there for dinner and that she'd moved out. After that, she said goodbye and left, just like that.

Brenna wanted to run after Cece and plead with her to stay. She wanted to cry out, "Don't leave me!" and throw her arms around her sister to hold her in place. As much as she wanted to beg, she knew that would just be babyish and make things even worse, so she held back.

After Cece left, her parents resumed their conversation. Her father wasn't shouting, as she'd expected, but his lowered voice was every bit as intimidating.

"This is unbelievable," her father said. "It's a slap in the face, considering everything I've done for her. You know that girl would be nowhere without me."

Her mother sighed. "I wouldn't take it personally, Harry. She's a young woman who wants to be on her own."

"Not take it personally?" He sounded outraged. "There's no other way to take it. And you know the worst part? She's going to botch the whole thing and come running back, begging for my help."

"Maybe not. Maybe it will be fine."

"It's not going to be fine. I've spent years building her brand, and now she decides to just tear it all down? We were so close to signing the reality show. That would have catapulted her to superstardom. Eventually she'd have a billion-dollar empire."

"Maybe that's not what she wants."

"Nonsense. That's what everybody wants, Deborah. Anyone who doesn't want it is an idiot." They were silent for a moment, and Brenna started backing away until she heard her father start up again. "You know who I blame?"

Her mom spoke quickly. "If you're going to say Greta, I have to say she's not at fault. She just got here, and she's such a sweet, quiet young woman that I can't imagine she could influence Cece that much in so short a time."

"Not Greta," her father said impatiently. "Definitely not Greta. I forgot all about her."

"Then who?"

"Nanny. She's always talking about following one's passion and how important it is to be true to yourself and work for the greater good." He harrumphed. "She's subliminally influencing our daughters with that garbage."

"I've never heard her say things like that."

"You would if you paid attention, Deborah."

"Now, dear, don't take it out on me. We're on the same team, remember?"

"Nanny doesn't know her place. She's been here too long and feels like she's part of the family."

"Brenna likes her, and she does a good job." Her mother spoke soothingly.

"For what we pay her, she *should* do a good job."

"Her salary is comparable to what other people pay their nannies. I think she's well worth it."

Her father coughed out a noise that said he didn't quite agree. "She may have been worth it when the girls were little, but how much work is it to take care of an eight-year-old? No diapers, no nighttime shifts, no bottles. Basically she's just here. I should have such an easy job."

"I think there's more to it than that. She helps to keep the staff on track and covers for us when we're out of town. When she's here, I don't need to worry."

Her father was having none of it. "Anyone could do her job. We pay her a significant salary, ask little of her, and what do we get in return? Insubordination."

"Insubordination? I'm afraid I don't understand," her mother said.

"She fills our daughters' heads with nonsense and undermines everything we've worked toward. I won't stand for it anymore. Nanny has to go."

"Go? Go where?"

"Out of this house. We'll give her two months' severance, of course, and a letter of recommendation. I'm not completely heartless."

"We can't fire Nanny," her mother said. She continued to

talk, making a case for keeping Nanny, but Brenna didn't catch most of the words because her heartbeat and breathing had accelerated, causing a rushing in her ears, and her legs began to move involuntarily, taking her out of her hiding spot and into the room where her parents sat.

"You can't fire Nanny!" she cried out, shocking herself and her parents too, who regarded her with wide eyes. "Who will take care of me?" She flung the stuffed dog down on the floor.

Her father spoke sharply. "That's enough, Brenna." He turned to her mother and pointed to the toy on the floor. "This kind of outburst illustrates my point perfectly. Nanny is not the disciplinarian we need her to be. I'll call her myself and let her know my decision."

Her mother pulled Brenna onto the couch next to her and said, "Wait a minute. Don't I get a say in the matter? Nanny is as much a friend as she is staff. She'd be very hard to replace. I say we give this a week or so before we make such a drastic decision."

This time it was her mother who got her father's famous glare. "My mind is made up, Deborah. You need to stop making friends with the help and start acting as their employer." He stood up and strode out of the room.

CHAPTER 3

*W*hen Cece closed the apartment door behind her, she leaned against it and let out a sigh. Up until that instant, she'd still thought her parents might come after her, her father demanding she return, her mother begging her to continue the conversation. Neither had happened. Making the break had been easier than she'd anticipated. Such a relief.

The sound of laughter came from the kitchen, and she followed the noise to find Dalton and Greta standing at the island, drink glasses in hand. Such a cute couple. If Cece hadn't known better, she'd have thought they'd been dating for months instead of days.

"You're back!" Dalton grinned.

"Do you want a mimosa?" Greta asked, holding up a pitcher of orange juice.

"A mimosa at one in the afternoon?"

Dalton said, "Mimosas are good anytime. What do you say? Are you in?"

"Yes, please." Cece sat on a stool and watched as Dalton got another glass and Greta gave her a generous amount of champagne before topping it off with orange juice. "Is that how they do it in Wisconsin?"

Greta laughed and said, "I think that's how everyone does it."

Cece took a sip. "I've had them when I was out to brunch. I never saw anyone make one before." There were so many ordinary things in life that had passed her by. She had a lot of catching up to do.

"How'd it go with your folks?" Greta asked. She and Dalton leaned against the counter, listening as Cece told them about the conversation with her parents. "I didn't even tell them I hired a new assistant, and I definitely didn't mention the meetings I have lined up." Cece had to fulfill some contractual obligations that were already in place, but after that, she had plans of her own. Her new line of designer clothes would actually be designed entirely by her, and she alone would pick out the material. The idea of choosing her own projects and having control over the decision-making was invigorating.

Greta was going to help, and Dalton was starting up a charitable organization to assist homeless veterans, so all of them were starting a new phase in their lives.

Cece said, "As I was leaving, my mom came after me, trying to smooth things over. She said that maybe I should let my dad be involved as a consultant, but I told her I was fine on my own." She took another sip of her mimosa. "I also told her Greta and I had moved into Vance and Kristina's old apartment." She took a look around. The apartment had been completely furnished, which made their move easier. A lot of the furnishings weren't to her taste, although that could easily be rectified. "I hope my dad doesn't make us move out."

"Oh, about that," Greta said brightly. "I have good news. I looked online at the tax records, and Firstborn Daughter Inc. is listed as the owner of this apartment, and there's no mortgage."

Cece regarded her blankly. "What does that mean?"

"It means *you* own the apartment in full, with no debt,"

Dalton said. "As long as you pay the property taxes, no one can make you move."

"Really?" She ran her finger around the rim of the glass. "You're right, that is good news." First her meeting with her parents went better than expected, and then she found out she owned a place to live. Added to that were her plans for the future, which now included seeing Roger. They'd met at the Forgotten Man Ball, and he was unlike all the men she'd crossed paths with so far.

Life was good, and things could only get better.

CHAPTER 4

*U*nable to stop the tears, Brenna burrowed her head against her mother's shoulder. Her mother made calming noises and rubbed her back. "It's okay, baby. It's all going to be okay."

Brenna relaxed against her mother, even as she knew the words rang false. Without Nanny, nothing would ever be okay again.

Brenna's mother waited until she had settled down and then suggested she put her new toy dog upstairs in her room. "If you could just hang out in your room for a bit, I need to go talk to Daddy about this Nanny situation," she explained gently. "He's just upset about Cece. I'm sure I can get him to change his mind. Don't worry, okay, darling?"

Brenna nodded and went to pick up the toy, then walked slowly up the stairs to her room, her mother alongside her. When her mother was so close, Brenna became even more aware of her extraordinary presence. Out of all the mothers of her classmates, hers was the most beautiful. She was tall and willowy, and she moved with the grace of a ballerina. Brenna liked to watch her get ready for an evening out. Watching her apply her makeup was like watching an artist at work. When she put her earrings in and slipped bracelets over her long fingers, her movements were swift and deliberate. Her mother instinctively knew how to coordinate her outfits, when to add a scarf or how to layer a cardigan. Which buttons to fasten and when to leave them open.

Sometimes after putting on her workout clothes, she pulled her hair up into a deliberate messy bun and secured it with a flash of her hands. Brenna had tried to do the same, but her hands were all fumbles and she didn't get the same results. Later, she'd told Cece that she thought she'd never measure up to their mother. "She always looks so perfect."

Cece said not to worry, that eventually she'd figure it out, but Brenna wasn't so sure. "Mom used to be a model, you know," her sister had said. "Back then her job was to look perfect. She's had a lot of practice." A job looking perfect. Brenna found old photos of her mother and couldn't believe how gorgeous she'd looked when she was in her twenties. Her sister was beautiful, but her mother was something else. She couldn't believe she'd ever match up to either of them. Only Nanny had been able to assuage her fears, pointing out that each person had talents of their own. Brenna didn't think she had any talents, but as if reading her mind, Nanny had said, "You, for instance, are an exceptional violin player for your age, and I've always been impressed that you practice without having to be reminded. That takes great discipline."

"But I don't mind practicing," Brenna had said. Did it count if she found it fun to do? It wasn't discipline so much as desire.

"That's just one of your talents," Nanny said. "And as you get older, you'll discover more. How a person looks is just a small part of who they are, but even so, you, my dear"—she paused to tap her on the nose—"are exceptionally beautiful. You have sparkling eyes and the best smile. Seeing your lovely face greet me in the morning is the best part of my day."

The best part of her day. Brenna believed it. Nanny's face did light up when she first saw Brenna, and she always acted happy to see her. Her parents were glad to see her too, but often they were on their way somewhere, or they were distracted, talking about business deals and people Brenna didn't know. Brenna had once heard one of the staff call her mom and dad "drive-by parents."

That was another good thing about Nanny. She never talked badly about other people. Everything she did was kind and loving.

When she and her mother got to the top of the stairs, Brenna veered off to her bedroom door while her mother kept going. She could hear her father's voice off in the distance, probably talking on the phone. His tone was serious but not angry, so maybe it was a business call and not a call to Nanny saying she was fired.

She sat on her bed, her back against the headboard, and tried to blink back the tears. If she had her cell phone, she could have called Nanny. But the cell phone was kept under lock and key and only given to her when she left the house, and only then under certain circumstances. Her father was old-school when it came to technology for his younger daughter. He looked old compared to most of the other dads, and he had old ideas to match. Her father definitely didn't believe children should go online unsupervised. She was the only one in her grade who didn't have a smartphone, something that was embarrassing.

Brenna was often lonely, but she couldn't remember ever having felt this alone. She didn't have a single person to tell her troubles to. In this household, she was currently the odd one out, the leftover. Her father had her mother. Greta had Dalton. Katrina had Vance, and of course they weren't even around anymore. And now Cece was seeing a man named Roger. All of them were in pairs.

But Brenna? Since Cece had moved out, Brenna only had Nanny. She couldn't imagine what her life would be like without her. It was too awful to think about.

CHAPTER 5

When Deborah entered the bedroom, Harry was pacing the floor, his cell phone in hand. She knew that look of nervous, anxious energy. Others might see his grim expression and the tightness in his shoulders and make the assumption he was angry. He so often came off that way, and there was some truth to it. His facade presented as anger, but underneath she knew that what presented as fury was actually disguised fear.

When they'd first gotten engaged, she'd heard what the gossips were saying. A young model from Wisconsin marrying a multimillionaire who came from old money? They had some choice words about the situation. She was described as a *gold digger, trophy wife, flavor of the month.* All of high society had an opinion. *Hope he has an airtight prenup. I give it a year!* Some of her relatives thought she'd struck it rich and had asked her for money, requests she'd ignored.

Only her father was able to assess the situation and cut right through outer appearances. Harry had told her years later that her dad had taken him aside at their engagement party and said,

"I have something to tell you, and you'd better listen up." He'd gestured to the other guests, all of them out of earshot. "You might be a big shot, rich and famous, owning half of Manhattan. All of these people think Deborah was the one who hit it lucky, but I'm here to tell you that *you're* the lucky one, and don't you forget it. Furthermore, if you ever hurt my daughter in any way, I will hunt you down and beat your sorry ass."

Harry, who never was at a loss for words, had been so taken aback that he'd only been able to mumble, "Yes, sir." Half an hour later, her father had made a toast to the newly engaged couple, wishing them a lifetime of happiness.

They had been happy, but it was a continuous balancing act. Only Deborah saw his anxiety. She knew it stemmed from his childhood. He'd endured the bullying of a verbally abusive alcoholic father and the trauma of his sister's death. She'd died of leukemia when he was a little boy, and Harry had never really gotten over the shock of losing her. The loss had made the world seem random in its cruelty. Trying to control everything around him was a coping mechanism, an effort to keep his life free from calamities.

Deborah knew she couldn't change him, so she worked with what she had, talking him through stressful times and coaching him on how to respond when he hit roadblocks in business. So often he wanted to lash out at those who didn't follow his directions, but because of her behind-the-scenes tutelage, he came up with better ways. Diplomacy was her strong suit.

Most of their friends had standing appointments with therapists. It was a thing among the moneyed of Manhattan, as routine as going to the dentist. Harry had often said he didn't need therapy because he had Deborah. Most people thought he was joking. He was not.

Seeing him pace, Deborah knew he was close to a meltdown. She'd have to proceed cautiously. "Everything's changing, isn't it?" She closed the door behind her. "I really hate it too."

He stopped walking. "Everything was under control with Cece. I had it all set up. She had work to keep her busy, multiple revenue streams, and the security of living at home. Now she's throwing it all away."

She went over and rested a hand on his arm. "I know it seems that way."

"It seems that way because it is that way."

Deborah exhaled. "If it makes you feel any better, she's not deliberately trying to undermine you. She's an adult. She wants to make her own decisions."

"We had a well-oiled machine here, Deborah." His words were tinged with frustration. "I've worked long and hard to create Cece's brand and persona. We were on the brink of a very big deal, and in the space of a few days, Katrina and Vance left, our daughter went out drinking and behaved disgracefully, and now she's refused to follow my plan."

"I saw the video, and it wasn't that disgraceful. If anything, I think it showed a fun, spontaneous side of our daughter."

"That video went viral and had millions of views. Everyone and their cousin has seen Cece looking like a drowned rat."

"The video has gotten mostly good comments." There was a long pause. "Harry, I don't think it's as big a deal as you think it is."

"If she wasn't happy, she could have said something. We could have worked out a better schedule or given her some vacation time."

"Maybe she didn't say anything because she didn't want to disappoint you or make you angry." She paused, letting the words work their way in. "I know you think this is a big disaster, but we'll get through this. You know that, right?"

He nodded, and the set of his shoulders relaxed.

She continued. "She's still our daughter, and she's living in Vance and Katrina's old apartment, so it's not like she's gone far. She still lives in our building, Harry."

"That's true. Maybe in a week or two she'll change her mind. Come to her senses." He ran his fingers through his hair. For a man his age, he had a surprisingly thick head of wavy hair, only slightly tinged with gray. The gossip mill speculated that it wasn't all his own. If they had bothered to ask Deborah, she could have assured them that every strand was original issue.

"Maybe she'll change her mind, but I think we should be prepared for that not to be the case. I think both of us will have an easier time of this if we accept that her life is completely out of our hands. We did the good work of raising her, and now it's up to Cece to decide what happens from here on out."

"Just like that?"

"Just like that. The same way you did at her age, and I did at an even younger age. I can tell you right now that I did not have my father's approval to move to New York and become a model, but I did it anyway, and look how it turned out. I found true love." She smiled, and the effect it had on him was a noticeable softening.

He gave her a thin-lipped smile and said, "Oh, Deborah, what would I do without you?"

"I hope you know how lucky you are to have me," she said, teasing.

"I do know." He brushed the hair back from her face and kissed her. "I really do."

"If you want to know the truth, I'm more worried about Brenna than Cece. She's such an anxious child, and Nanny is *so* good with her." She tried to read his face. "I like that we can travel knowing that we're leaving our daughter in the hands of someone so capable and caring."

"If she's so capable, why did everything fall apart while we were gone?"

"You can hardly blame Nanny for what happened with Cece."

"You know me better than that. Knowing who to blame is one of life's most important skills."

He said the words in a grumpy way, but she detected a lightening behind the gloom. She tapped his chest with a manicured fingernail. "Do you really want me to hire someone new? We'd have to have the agency send over applicants, and there would be interviews and checking their references and drug testing. And we'd have to get used to someone new. It's always such an ordeal, and why? Nanny has been an outstanding employee. She never calls in sick, and she loves our girls."

"Maybe too much. She could be a lot stricter, in my opinion."

"And she's discreet. We can trust her not to betray what happens in this household."

"She signed a contract. She has to be discreet or she'll get sued."

"Well, now you're just arguing for sport." Deborah let out a breathless laugh, sensing that she'd turned his mood. She wrapped her arms around his neck, and he leaned down so their foreheads touched. Giving him a quick kiss, she said, "You don't really want to fire Nanny, do you?"

He cleared his throat, and his voice came out strong and clear. "I already did. I called and left a voice message saying she was no longer employed here and that she should contact my assistant to find out the details of her severance package."

"Hmm." She reached up and stroked his cheek, waiting until he gave the small smile of defeat she knew was forthcoming. It took a minute, but there it was. Despite his best efforts, there was a slight upturning of his lips. She knew him so well. Clearly, he'd regretted being so rash, but she knew from past experience that he would never admit it. Once again, she'd have to come to his rescue. She whispered, "I'll call her back and tell her it was a misunderstanding and she still has a job."

He sighed and nodded. "If that's what you want."

"It's what I want."

"Since you feel so strongly about it, I'll let you take care of it."

Deborah said, "I think I'll also tell her she's getting a bonus with her next paycheck because Mr. Vanderhaven and I appreciate her many years of devotion to our family."

CHAPTER 6

*C*urious, Brenna stuck her head out of the doorway, listening to the quiet hum of her parents' conversation from down the corridor. She tried to make out what they were talking about. Her father was a little louder than her mother, but even his words were hard to make out. She had to know what was going on. Her mother had been clear in telling her to stay in her room, and Brenna understood that the grown-ups didn't want her around when they were arguing. It was bad enough when they had disagreements about other things, but this time it was about her and her life.

She would, she decided, just take a quick listen and then sneak back to her room. They'd never even know she was there.

The hallway runner muffled the sound of her footsteps, but she went slowly anyway, their voices becoming clearer as she got closer. With her ear against the door, she heard her mother say, "You don't really want to fire Nanny, do you?"

Her father cleared his throat. "I already did. I called and left a voice message saying she was no longer employed here and that she should contact my assistant to find out the details of her severance package."

She waited a moment, but her mother didn't say anything. Brenna knew that when her father did something, there was no turning back. There was no undoing it. He'd never admit he made a mistake.

So it was final. She was never going to see Nanny again. Brenna's eyes filled with tears. Nanny had never been anything but caring and kind to everyone in the household. Why was her father blaming her for something she had no part of? It just wasn't fair. She turned around and went back down the hall, not even trying to be quiet, but her parents didn't come out of their room. She was sadder than she'd ever been in her entire life, and no one even noticed. She had no one to tell her troubles to, no one to talk her through her grief.

Her heart felt like it was being squeezed. This, she realized, must be what it was like to be brokenhearted. She sat on her bed cross-legged, letting the tears drop onto her legs. After a few minutes, she wiped her eyes with the back of her hand and went into the bathroom to blow her nose. Looking into the mirror, she saw a girl who had no one. The saddest girl in the world. She would give anything to have Nanny right there in her room, telling her everything was going to be fine. She hoped that Nanny didn't blame her for getting fired. Would she think Brenna had said something, maybe complained about her?

The idea that Nanny might think she could be the cause of her pain made her sick inside. She had to set the record straight. But how? She was allowed a cell phone only under certain circumstances. Even if she was able to get hold of someone else's, she didn't know Nanny's number.

Pushing off the bed, she left her room, closing the door behind her, and went to the stairwell. Once downstairs, she paused while one of the maids walked past, carrying a handheld vacuum cleaner. Once she was out of sight, Brenna left the apartment and got into the elevator.

This small act, leaving without permission, would be

perceived as rebellion and could get her grounded for a month. Her parents were firm in that she could only leave the apartment with an adult. Being in the elevator by herself, something simple but forbidden, was both freeing and terrifying. For a split second, she considered going back, then dismissed the notion. She pushed the button to what used to be Vance and Katrina's floor, and the elevator skimmed downward, the numbers flashing as it went. When it stopped and the doors slid open, Brenna got out and went straight to Cece's new apartment. Music was playing inside. She raised her hand to knock on the door but stopped when she heard a man's voice, followed by laughing. The laughter, which had now turned into something like shrieking, sounded like her sister, along with their cousin Greta. She listened a bit longer and heard what sounded like the clinking of glasses followed by the man saying he was making a toast to Cece's new life. Greta cried out, "Here, here," or maybe she was saying, "Hear, hear."

Brenna's brow furrowed in puzzlement. She'd never known her sister to laugh like that. The only way this made sense was if Cece was having a party. The man's voice had to be that Roger that Cece was always texting. Or maybe it was Dalton, the guy who had a thing for their cousin Greta. Suddenly, she felt too shy to interrupt. She'd wanted to have her sister all to herself; she hadn't been counting on there being others in the apartment. She swallowed, gearing up to knock, and raised her hand tentatively. Inside she heard Cece laughing again. Brenna pressed her ear against the door, thinking she could hear more. The conversation was still slightly muffled, until she heard Cece saying quite clearly, "Ugh, I'm so happy to be free of my family."

Another female voice (Greta's?) shouted, "To freedom!"

Brenna felt her stomach drop. Cece didn't want to be bothered with her anymore. Her hand fell to her side, and she glanced back at the elevator, the doors of which still stood open. As they began to slide shut, she made a split-second decision and charged back, her hand grabbing the edge of the door as it slid closed.

Once the doors shut, she pressed the button for the lobby. She'd already left the apartment; going a little farther wouldn't make it any worse. When the door opened, one of the women behind the front desk spotted her and said, "Good afternoon, Miss Vanderhaven."

They always knew her, these women behind the desk. They were all pretty, with tidy hair and crisp white shirts and navy-blue vests. Their uniforms reminded her of what flight attendants wore in old movies. Since they were familiar with her, Brenna felt like she should know their names, but there were so many of them, and they changed all the time. She quietly answered, "Good afternoon." And then, because she didn't know what else to do, she walked toward the front door. The doorman, who had to be new because she'd never seen him before, opened it for her with a smile. "Good afternoon, miss. By yourself today?"

She nodded. Out on the sidewalk, she blinked in the afternoon sun. Without Nanny or her mother next to her, she felt the same way she did when her hair wasn't parted on the correct side. Something wasn't right, something that was apparent only to her. On the sidewalk in front of her, a couple wearing workout attire pushed a stroller with giant wheels. A fat-cheeked toddler strapped inside the stroller held a plush bunny and a sippy cup. Down the block a cab pulled to the curb, letting out a businessman carrying a black leather briefcase. People came and went, but no one seemed interested in Brenna. She waited for the paparazzi who sometimes descended on her sister and scanned the street for the kidnappers her father was sure would snatch her if she ever went outside unaccompanied.

Nothing happened. The sky overhead was blue with white puffy clouds. The street sights and sounds were the same as they ever were: horns blaring while a messenger bike wove in and out of traffic. The doorman came up from behind her and touched her shoulder, startling her. "Can I help you with something, miss?"

She saw now that his name tag said "Cooper" and that he had a concerned look on his face. "No, I'm fine," she said. "Just going for a walk around the block."

"Very good," he said. "You picked a marvelous day for it." With the flat of his hand he gave her an approving salute.

Such a weird thing to say, Brenna thought as she walked away. As if she'd picked the day for the walk instead of the other way around. She took a few tentative steps, then got bolder, heading in the direction Nanny always went when she'd taken Brenna to her home in Brooklyn. Nanny's place was much smaller than the Vanderhaven apartment and somewhat cluttered, with recipes and photos tacked to the refrigerator with magnets, but Brenna had found it cozy and inviting. She especially loved playing with Nanny's two cats. She and Nanny had gone to her home in Brooklyn several times over the years, always taking the subway and walking the last stretch, which went on for many blocks. Once they'd even walked over the bridge, something that Nanny thought every New Yorker should do at least once. At the time she'd told Brenna, "One of these days we should walk the bridge in the evening, when the sun is just going down. That's really a spectacular sight." They'd had so many plans, so many things left unfinished.

Brenna headed in the general direction of the subway entrance that would eventually get her to Brooklyn. The subway had maps posted, and she could always ask people for help. By looking for familiar landmarks, she was fairly certain she could figure it out as she went along.

CHAPTER 7

*a*n hour after he'd left the voice mail telling the nanny she was fired, Harry rapped on Brenna's bedroom door. Deborah thought it would be best for him to tell their younger daughter that he'd made a mistake and that Nanny would not be leaving their employment. His wife had suggested that he explain it in the context of being worried about Cece, that he'd overreacted and that upon second thought, he had changed his mind.

This idea of parents admitting their faults was alien to Harry. He'd always believed that a parent's infallibility was the bedrock of security for their offspring. So much of life was scary and prone to change. Knowing they had a father who was constant and steady had to be reassuring to his offspring. Why in heaven's name would he admit to having made a bad decision?

Deborah thought he took this philosophy to extremes, and maybe she was right. When it came to business, his instincts were spot-on. When it came to people, especially those around him, he'd learned to follow his wife's lead. She was truly his better half. Without her in his life, he knew he would be lost.

When Brenna didn't respond to his knock, he spoke through the door. "Brenna, it's Dad. Can I come in?" Even hearing himself say those words was a bit galling. It was his house—of course he could go in. It wasn't like he needed the permission of an eight-year-old.

This issue of privacy had first been raised when Cece was about six or seven and Deborah had instructed him that she was entitled to her sense of personal space. "Girls don't want their dad walking in when they're getting dressed or doing something silly," she'd said. "It's not that big of a deal to knock. You're a gentleman—you know the importance of respecting a lady's space." It made sense once she put it that way. He'd been thinking of Cece as their baby, not a young woman in the making.

"Brenna?" He opened the door a crack, only to see the room was completely dark, the shades drawn against the sunlight. She must be taking a nap. He spoke through the two-inch opening in the door. "Are you sleeping?" He waited for an instant before continuing. "Listen, I just wanted to let you know that I thought better of my decision and have reversed my position on the matter. Nanny will still continue to work for us."

He'd bypassed the part about making a mistake. It was easier that way. "So you don't need to worry. Everything is going to continue the way it always has. And Cece will be living just downstairs, I made sure of that." In a way it was true since he'd arranged for Cece's company, Firstborn Daughter Inc., to buy the apartment. Why would Cece move anywhere else if she already owned a unit in one of the best buildings in Manhattan? Knowing he'd been able to provide a home for his older daughter and reassure his youngest all in one afternoon made Harry feel uncharacteristically emotional. "Okay, honey, just take a little nap. We'll talk later." He closed the door carefully and stood in the hallway, listening to see if she stirred. When he didn't hear anything after a minute, he returned to the bedroom to report back to Deborah.

Deborah was on the phone with Nanny when he walked in, her back to the door. "Yes, that's right. Harry misunderstood something that had occurred here while we were gone. Both of us feel terrible about the voice mail message you received. We were a little jet-lagged and worried about Cece, as you can imagine." She listened for a long time and then chuckled. "Of course. I'm so glad you understand."

Turning, his wife acknowledged his presence with one raised finger. She nodded and smiled as she turned her attention back to the phone. "Oh! And one other thing. Because you're so important to our family and have been working for us for so long, Harry and I have decided to add a two-thousand-dollar bonus to your next paycheck."

Harry gasped and mouthed the words *Two thousand dollars?*

She waved off his objections. "No, we insist. It's our pleasure. Truly." After she wrapped up the conversation and clicked off, she turned to him and said, "How'd it go with Brenna?"

He gave her a smile. "Just fine, I think. She was taking a nap, so I didn't barge in and disturb her. I just opened the door a bit and told her that Nanny would be staying on."

Deborah surveyed him suspiciously. "You told her you made a mistake?"

"More or less."

"Hmm." She knew him so well. "And did you end the conversation by telling her you love her?"

"She knows I love her."

"Oh, Harry." She shook her head. "You are such a work in progress."

He took her in his arms. "I never said it would be easy."

"No, that's true, you never did."

CHAPTER 8

$\mathcal{O}$nce Brenna made it to the subway entrance, she followed a herd of people down the steps. Most of them, she guessed, were coming from the museum. To her relief, a subway map was posted on the wall at the bottom of the stairs. She studied it and figured out she needed to be on the F train, then realized she had no MetroCard. Brenna checked her pockets even though she knew they were empty. *Shoot!* If only she'd thought to bring some money. Maybe someone would lend her some? She tried to catch the eye of the motherly-looking types without success, then scanned the ground, thinking she might find lost coins. She was about to give up when she noticed a young guy hop over the turnstile. When no one objected, she followed suit, ducking under the bar. Her heart pounded at the thought she might be caught breaking the law. On the other side, she waited for someone to notice, certain she'd get in trouble. But, no. The other passengers took no notice of her. Everyone, it seemed, was concentrating on their own destination. Even a baby, strapped to its mother's front, seemed indifferent.

On the subway there were other kids around her age, some

of whom seemed to be traveling alone. Why had she never noticed this the other times she'd ridden with Nanny? For some reason, she'd thought it was a rule that a grown-up had to accompany a child on public transportation.

She sat down at the end of a row right near the door, gripping the silver handrail next to her seat. Just before the doors slid shut, a man with neatly combed hair, dark glasses, and a backpack barreled through and took the seat next to hers. As the doors came together, he shifted uncomfortably closer. She didn't make eye contact with him, but shifted away from him. There was a foot of space available on the other side of him, so why was he sitting so close and crowding her? If Nanny was here, she'd ask him to move down, but Brenna wasn't that bold. Besides, she'd gotten on without a ticket, so she wasn't even a paying passenger. Did she have a right to make a fuss?

Still aware of his presence, she turned her head and looked away from him, studying a baby with three fingers stuck in its mouth, a string of drool dropping onto the front of his mother's shirt. He made sucking on those fingers look like a serious job. She smiled at him, and he regarded her blankly.

The man leaned down, talking into her ear. "Nice day, huh?" She could smell his coffee breath and see the unshaven stubble on his face.

She nodded but didn't move. She wasn't sure why her heart began to race. He didn't look scary. If anything, he looked like someone's dad heading home from work. Nanny had gone over stranger danger when she was just a little kid, and they discussed it periodically. The word *inappropriate* came up every time. This felt inappropriate, but she couldn't quite put her finger on why. His tone was friendly, and he wasn't saying anything that caused alarm.

"Would you, by chance, have a cell phone I could borrow?" Again, his voice was right in her ear. Brenna had the feeling that if she turned her head she'd smack into his face.

"Me?" She leaned as far away from him as she could and turned just enough to see him. "No, I don't have a cell phone with me."

"Ah, too bad," he said. "Mine is dead, and I wanted to call my friend. We're supposed to meet up, but I'm running late. I do hate being late. Plus, I don't want him to worry."

She looked down at her shoes. Maybe if she ignored him, he'd leave her alone.

No such luck. He kept on, saying, "You remind me of my niece, Gracie." He laughed, but it sounded forced. "Oh yes, Gracie does love her uncle Luke. You two must be around the same age. She's seven. How old are you?"

A personal question. Nanny had said she never had to answer a stranger's personal questions, although this one seemed not too bad. Out of the corner of her eye, she saw him waiting expectantly. Finally, she said, "I'm older than that." She was proud of her response. She had been polite but hadn't really given him any information.

"Wow, big girl, huh? Is someone with you today, or are you riding the subway alone?"

Panic and fear bloomed in her chest. His mouth was so close she could see his chapped lips.

She didn't answer, and he kept on. "Not saying there's anything wrong with kids riding the subway by themselves. I think it's great that you're so independent and adventurous. A lot of girls your age wouldn't be."

The car slowed as it approached the next stop. In anticipation, people pushed closer to the door. A young woman, her hair artfully arranged in braids crisscrossed atop her head, held on to the very same pole Brenna was clutching. Her legs were so close they were nearly against Brenna's knees.

He tried again. "Do your folks know where you are?"

Anguished, Brenna glanced upward to the woman, mentally asking for help. The woman immediately sized up the situation.

She said, "Do you know this man?" Brenna shook her head, and the woman said, "Stop creeping on little girls, you perv!"

"I was just making conversation," he said, putting up his hands in defense. "Sue me for being friendly."

"I'm going to do a whole lot more than that if you bother this child again." She leaned over and said to Brenna, "I have to go, but there are open seats right over there." She pointed. "Don't be afraid to move if someone's bothering you. Don't give him that power." She wagged a finger at the man. "You mind your manners, sir."

"I didn't do anything," he muttered under his breath.

She helped Brenna to her feet, then stretched out an arm to clear the way for her as the car lurched to a stop. When the doors opened, Brenna moved against the current of people. Because she was small and nimble, she was able to weave through the throng to an empty seat thirty feet away. She settled into a seat next to an elderly woman who held a book on her lap. As the car moved forward, she looked out the window to see the woman who'd helped her, now walking at a fast clip. She didn't glance up to see Brenna's wave.

After a few minutes, the old lady next to her asked where she was going. Although this sounded like a personal question, it didn't feel inappropriate coming from this silver-haired woman, and so Brenna answered, "Park Slope, Brooklyn, to visit my nanny."

"Aren't you a sweet granddaughter! I bet she'll love a visit."

Brenna didn't correct her, just nodded politely when the woman started telling her about her own granddaughter, showing her photos on her phone. "Delia loves to play with my cat." She showed her a picture of the girl carrying a big white fluffball of a cat. "Her mother is allergic," she said in a whisper, as if speaking confidentially.

"My nanny has two cats," she said. "Fanta and Smokey. They're really cute. Fanta does tricks." Somehow, Nanny had trained the old orange cat to play fetch using milk carton rings. It was a game both Fanta and Brenna loved. Besides playing fetch, Fanta would jump really high when someone held up a cat treat. Although maybe that wasn't technically a trick because she really loved her treats.

"I'm guessing that Fanta is an orange cat and Smokey is gray?" The woman smiled, and Brenna noticed her face was as wrinkled as a crumpled paper bag, and her silvery gray hair had been pulled back into a messy ponytail. None of that mattered, really, because when she smiled, all Brenna saw was the kindness in her eyes.

"That's right. Fanta is really fat, but Smokey is kind of little. Sometimes they sleep together." Fanta often slept with her paw thrown over Smokey's back, like they were people.

"You don't have a cat yourself?"

"No." She shook her head. "No pets. I would love to have a dog, but my dad thinks it's a bad idea."

"Oh, well. It's hard to have a dog in the city." She clucked sympathetically and patted Brenna's arm. "At least you have cats at your grandmother's house." When the subway car lurched to a stop and the doors slid open, the woman said, "This is Park Slope, dear. Is this your stop?"

"Yes." Brenna stood up to join the crowd getting ready to exit the car.

"Have a good visit," the woman called out from behind her.

"I will, thanks."

CHAPTER 9

*T*he Vanderhavens stood in the lobby, questioning the doorman, Cooper, for what seemed like the hundredth time, as if his answer might change in the retelling. He told them, "She was by herself. I asked if she needed help, and she said no, that she was taking a walk around the block." He sounded composed, but underneath his calm demeanor he was quaking. His first day on the job and already he'd made an enormous blunder, and with one of the most prestigious families in Manhattan. Mentally he could have kicked himself for being so careless. *Idiot!* What was he thinking?

His girlfriend, Tabitha, had joked about everything he'd gone through to land this position: a round of three different interviews, drug testing, legal clearance involving fingerprinting, the necessity of providing multiple references, and testing for both manners and intelligence. "You'd think you were going to work for the CIA," she'd said.

"It might just be a doorman position, but it's an entry into other opportunities," he'd said. He'd been given a manual with rules for his personal conduct, along with a listing of what was expected of him while at his post. He'd memorized the names and faces of everyone who lived in the building and what their expectations would be. The manager had clued him in on some of their idiosyncrasies as well. One female resident, a bestselling novelist, did not like to be greeted with anything more than a nod. Talking, she said, interrupted her train of thought, something that was essential for her line of work. Another resident, an older man, loved to be fussed over and admired, so compliments were always welcome. Yet another was a bit of a hypochondriac and thrived on sympathy. Cooper had memorized all this and more, but nowhere did it say that an eight-year-old girl couldn't go outside by herself.

He knew about the Vanderhavens, of course. One of the women who worked the front desk had said the husband was grouchy, the wife sweet but aloof, and the daughters polite. He had wondered about Brenna being all alone when she came off the elevator, but it was not his place to stop her. And then after she'd left, he'd gotten busy with other tasks. He would have forgotten about the incident completely if not for her parents rushing out of the elevator and interrogating him.

Harry Vanderhaven said, "So she just walked away, and you watched her go." He gestured toward the door. "Not a thought in your head that this might be a problem?"

Cooper squirmed as he realized there was no good answer. Truthfully, he hadn't watched her go for very long, Instead, he'd gone back inside and returned to work. He said, "She declined my assistance and said she wanted to take a walk. Around the block."

"So you said." Harry crossed his arms and scowled at him. "And you didn't think it was odd that she didn't come back forty-five minutes later? How long does it take *you* to walk around the block?"

Cooper was pretty sure he was going to lose his job anyway, so he threw decorum aside and just came out with what he was thinking. "Regardless of my decision, which I acknowledge was a poor one, the truth of the matter is that she's still gone." What he didn't say was that haranguing the doorman would not bring her back. "I'm sure she's fine, but if this were my daughter, I'd be making some phone calls to her friends. Failing that, I think a call to the police is in order."

Cooper saw the look of anger on Mr. Vanderhaven's face build; the man seemed to get physically larger as well. He took a step back, anticipating a blow, but Mrs. Vanderhaven rested a hand on her husband's arm and said, "He's right, Harry. It doesn't sound like she's been abducted, but she could be lost. She doesn't have her phone, and I don't think she had any money with her. We need to make some calls and get the authorities involved."

"If this man had stopped her, it never would have gotten to that point."

"Everyone makes mistakes, Harry. *Everyone.*"

"The kind of mistake that loses our daughter?"

"It's his first day on the job. He didn't know. Everyone makes mistakes."

Cooper got the impression they'd covered this topic before. Hearing his wife's words, Mr. Vanderhaven's shoulders slumped and he sighed. "As usual, you're right, Deborah."

She addressed Cooper. "We know it's not your fault that she walked out, but for future reference, Brenna is not allowed to leave the building unaccompanied. Our family is publicly known, and not everyone is friendly. I'm sure you understand."

Cooper nodded. He did understand. Good grief, he hoped Brenna had just gone to a friend's house. If she'd been kidnapped, he would never forgive himself. "Thank you for being so understanding. If it helps, I do know the direction she went, and the outdoor security cameras will confirm it as well. Would you like me to call the police on your behalf? We can caution them not to make a scene."

"Thank you, we'd appreciate that," Harry said.

The couple nodded. Deborah opened the clasp to her handbag and took out her phone. It had a large screen and a glittery gold cover. She tapped on the screen and put it up to her ear. "Cece, it's Mom. You need to come down to the lobby right now. Brenna's missing."

CHAPTER 10

$\mathcal{G}$reta and Dalton accompanied Cece down to the lobby, where Cece's mom was waiting to fill them in. "Your father said she was napping, so I thought I'd let her sleep. I wish I had checked on her," she said, her voice tight with regret. "Later when I didn't find her in her room, I assumed she was somewhere else in the apartment, so we had everyone stop what they were doing and help us search." Cece knew that by *everyone* she meant the staff. She imagined the cook putting down her ladle and helping to hunt for her sister, the maids abandoning their vacuum cleaners and dustcloths and walking from room to room, calling out Brenna's name. "We tore the whole apartment apart—every room, closet, cabinet, everything—and she was just gone. Gone!" She wrung her hands in worry.

"It's going to be okay," Cece said. Seeing her normally cool, elegant mother in a near state of hysteria was completely out of character.

Her mother kept going. "I tried calling Nanny, but she didn't pick up, so I left a voice mail. I talked to her earlier and she didn't mention Brenna, so I doubt she's heard from her."

"She would have called if she'd heard from Brenna," Cece said.

"The next thing we did was check with the front desk. That's when we found out she left the building to go for a walk. By herself!"

"I can't imagine what she was thinking," her dad said. He blinked and looked away. For a second Cece thought she saw a glint of tears in his eyes.

"She wouldn't have just left without a good reason," Cece said. "Something had to have happened. I know she wasn't thrilled with the toy you brought her from Paris. Could that have been it?"

"I don't think so. It was really nothing to get upset about." Her mother waved her hand in dismissal. "A minor disappointment."

Cece pondered for a moment. "Maybe she was upset that I moved out? She is a sensitive child."

Her mother sighed. "That could be it. Whatever it is, we just need to find her."

"Can't they trace the GPS on her phone?" Dalton asked. He had his arm around Greta's shoulder. Greta's look of anxiety mirrored Cece's own feelings.

She shook her head. "She didn't have her phone, and we don't think she had any money on her either. It's like she just impulsively walked out of the apartment and left for no reason at all."

Outside, two squad cars pulled up to the curb. In a few minutes, two police officers and a pair of detectives were in the lobby, taking names and asking her parents for a timeline of Brenna's disappearance.

Disappearance. The word was fully charged with terror and permanence. Cece couldn't bear to think of her sister out in the world, alone and lost, or worse yet, having been kidnapped or abducted. Brenna was raised in Manhattan and was no stranger to navigating crowds. Still, she was shy and used to having Nanny or a family member with her when she was out in public. Without an adult, a phone, or money, she'd be in a bad way.

Cece had to admit, too, that Brenna was on the babyish side of her age group, not nearly as sophisticated as most of her classmates. The same had been true of Cece for most of her life, and she blamed her parents for that. They kept their daughters sheltered and cut off from so much of what was going on in the world. In Cece's case, ironically enough, she was kept away from the world right up until her father decided her life path would be that of a social media celebrity, thus thrusting her right into the very world he'd shielded her from all along. Such a mistake. Cece vowed that when she had kids, she'd do things very differently. She'd most likely just be making entirely different mistakes, but at least her children wouldn't go through the same trials she had.

Detective Thompson asked if he could send the two officers up to search the apartment and look for clues in Brenna's room. "It's standard procedure," he said. Her mother murmured her assent, while her father looked dumbstruck.

"If you want, we can take them up," Greta said cautiously.

"I think that's a good idea," Cece said, and when neither of her parents objected, Dalton and Greta took the lead, heading toward the elevator with the officers in tow.

"Can you tell us what she was wearing?" Detective Zagon asked, ready to write it down.

Deborah looked at her husband, who shrugged. She squinted, trying to recall. "Jeans? I think she was wearing jeans."

Cece stepped forward. "She was wearing a cream-colored top with a scooped neck and navy shorts with slip-on canvas shoes. Tan. The shoes were tan."

The next request was for a recent photo of Brenna. Both of Cece's parents took out their phones, but neither of them could find any pictures of their daughters. Looking over her mother's shoulder, Cece watched as her mother scrolled past images from France: beautiful artwork, high-end hotels, gourmet meals, and luminescent cocktails. "We just got back from a trip to Paris," her mother said apologetically.

"I usually just take work photos," her dad said, explaining why most of his pictures were of buildings he was considering buying.

Cece reached into her bag and pulled out her phone, then found a picture taken the previous week of the two of them together. That afternoon Greta had commented on the sisters' resemblance, and Cece had taken a selfie with Brenna to compare. They did look alike, especially in the way they smiled. "Will this work?" she asked, handing it over.

"Perfect," Detective Thompson said. "We'll have to crop you out," he added.

"Of course."

Now that the police were involved, Cece should have felt better. Instead, it was all the worse because it seemed official. Before the cops had arrived, her sister had just gone for a walk. Now she was *missing*. Too, Cece was going out of her skin with the way the police were wasting valuable time asking the same questions over and over again. They wanted to know about drug use, something that perplexed Cece until she realized they were asking about *Brenna*. Brenna using drugs? It was unthinkable. The one time their mother had let Brenna take a sip of her wine, she had all but spit it out. No, she assured them, there was no drug usage. No online boyfriend who could have talked her into an illicit meeting. There was no way she could have become involved in a group or cult online or in real life. She was eight years old, going on seven.

"She's really such a baby," Cece said, trying to explain. "Very innocent for her age. She still believes in Santa."

The officer gave her a weary smile. "I'm sorry, but we have to ask these questions. You'd be surprised how often family members don't know what their children are up to."

After they'd interviewed the doorman and searched the ground floor, including the basement and back exit, Cece and her parents and the detectives went up to the apartment. There were more questions, and then they asked to take the laptop Brenna used for homework. Her mother nodded and went to get it from her bedroom. When she got back, they requested the phone numbers of Brenna's teachers and closest friends, which her mom managed to find as well.

Her father, who had been strangely silent, finally spoke up. "Why aren't you on the street looking for my daughter? It's getting later and later . . ." He cast a glance at the window, his voice breaking. "God only knows what's happened to her."

"We're doing everything we can, Mr. Vanderhaven," Detective Zagon said. "We have officers on the street looking for her now, and others are surveying security cameras in the area. It all takes time, but believe me, we are searching for your daughter."

"I don't want this made public," Dad said quietly. "Splashing the story all over the news will just attract a bad element that would prey on her if they find her."

"A bad element?" Cece had trouble assigning meaning to the words. Did he mean that the enemies of the Vanderhaven Corporation, those who'd lost their jobs during mergers or were outbid in business dealings, would do something horrible to her sister? Or worse, did he think actual criminals would come upon Brenna and kidnap and torture her? Both thoughts were too terrible to think about.

"I'm sorry, but making this public is our best bet for finding your daughter. Your daughter doesn't fit the criteria for an AMBER Alert, because there's been no indication that she's endangered, but I would suggest we activate a Missing Child Alert. That way, Brenna's information can be distributed electronically to all the surrounding police agencies, as well as toll barriers, travel plazas, and broadcasters. It also goes out to anyone who subscribes to these kinds of alerts. It is different from an AMBER Alert, because the station managers of media outlets make the decision as to whether or not to air the alert."

"Don't they usually wait forty-eight hours?" he asked, sounding dismayed.

"Sir, that's for adults or teenagers. An eight-year-old alone in the city could be at risk, especially given how well known your family is," Detective Zagon said.

"But she could walk in the door at any moment."

"And if she does, we'll call off the alert. From my experience, these kinds of alerts are valuable. They save lives."

Her father reluctantly acquiesced. "If you think it's absolutely necessary."

"I do." His tone was matter-of-fact. "You should be aware, sir, that the news of your daughter going missing would probably come out regardless. I'm sure other people overheard us in the lobby, and you have employees who know as well—"

"My employees would never tell."

Detective Zagon nodded. "Still, things tend to get out, so it's best to get ahead of it. It might be helpful for you to have a statement prepared."

"We've always been a private family, but if it will help bring Brenna home, of course we'll do whatever you say." Her father took her mother's hand, and she nodded in agreement.

A private family? Cece thought back to how he'd propelled her in front of the world's eye, having cameras follow her everywhere she went. Apparently, the privacy only applied to him.

Detective Zagon said, "I think it's best."

CHAPTER 11

*A*fter the police left, Cece's dad sank down onto the sofa, still clutching Detective Thompson's business card. "I feel like I should be doing something," he said, frustrated. "I just don't know what to do." He set the card down and cradled his head in his hands. Her mother sat down next to him and patted his back.

Cece had never seen him so overcome with emotion. As she was growing up, it was rare to hear him say he loved her or Brenna. As a parent, he was often absent, and when he was home, it was hard to engage him. Over the years, she'd try to talk to him, telling him about friends or a good grade she'd gotten on a school project, and he listened politely, but it was clear his mind was usually elsewhere. *Disinterested* was the word that came to mind. As if he were tolerating his daughter. Her mother had justified his behavior with a variety of excuses. He was busy, distracted by the stresses of work. He wasn't a warm, hugging type of dad. His own childhood had been lacking in affection.

Her mother had assured the girls that he was trying, he really was. He just found it difficult.

48

Until now, Cece had thought it was just a line, something to help them get over the fact that they had an inattentive father. She always felt their presence was welcome only if he could brag about them. Otherwise, they were an inconvenience.

Now before her eyes he'd suddenly transformed into a sad little boy, unsure and afraid. Worried that he'd lost his daughter.

Greta and Dalton stood off to one side of the room, available to help but not wanting to interfere.

Her father said, "They said to sit here and wait in case she comes back. I feel like I should be looking for her, but what could I do that the police can't? I don't know. I just don't know what to do."

As he talked, a plan formed in Cece's mind. With complete clarity, it came to her in bullet points, making perfect sense. "*I know what to do.*" She spoke authoritatively, the certainty in her voice surprising even herself. Gesturing for Greta and Dalton to come in closer, she continued. "The Missing Child Alert is a good start, but we need to get more sets of eyes searching for Brenna. If we go wide with this, we can cover all of Manhattan." She'd learned the term *going wide* from her father's business talk, something she knew would put her plan in his favor. "If I post on all my social media outlets, we can spur my followers into immediate action." She snapped her fingers for emphasis. "My fans will search for her like you would not believe, and if I offer an evening with Cece Vanderhaven and her family to anyone who helps to bring her home, we won't attract the weirdos who come sniffing around when you offer monetary rewards."

Her mother sat up and gave Cece a look of surprised admiration. "I think this is an excellent idea."

Cece said, "Secondly, we'll try calling Nanny one more time, and if she still doesn't answer, Greta and Dalton will go to her house to try to reach her in person. Nanny might have some idea of where Brenna would have gone." If anyone would know, it would be Nanny.

"We're on it," Greta said, and Dalton nodded.

"Mom and I will stay in the apartment in case Brenna returns. We'll call the detectives and let them know we're using my social media channels, and then Mom and I will monitor the comments on my accounts to see if anyone has seen Brenna. Dad, while we're doing that, you can walk the neighborhood and look for her. She might be afraid of the police, but if she sees you or hears your voice, it would be a different matter." She looked around the room. "We'll all keep updated by text." She got out her phone. "I'll send everyone a photo of Brenna that you can use when asking people if they've seen her."

Her father looked to her mother. "You think this is a good idea, Deborah?"

"Absolutely." She leaned in and kissed his cheek. "Cece has all these resources. We might as well use them."

"All right, then, we'll let Cece take the lead on this one."

Take the lead on this one. That was another phrase from her dad's book of corporate talk, and this time Cece found it especially appropriate. She was taking the lead. No longer the girl who did what she was told, she was now a woman who made things happen.

Her mother tried calling Nanny once more but still didn't get through, then called the police to let them know what they'd be doing. While her mother was punching in the detective's number, Greta and Dalton headed out to Brooklyn to Nanny's place with a promise to call back after they'd arrived.

Her father left the apartment right after her mother spoke to the police. Just before heading out, he said, "You'll let me know if you hear anything?"

"The very minute," Cece promised, holding the door for him. After he got on the elevator, she joined her mother in the living room and turned on her tablet.

50

Her mom asked, "Did you mean what you said—that Brenna might be afraid to go to the police but would respond to your dad's voice?"

"That was part of it," Cece said, her eyes still on the screen. "But I also thought Dad needed something to do."

"Really." Her mother regarded her thoughtfully. "You're right about that. When did you get to be so smart?"

Cece paused thoughtfully. "I think I've always been smart. I was just afraid to show it."

She returned her attention to the tablet, cropping the photo of Brenna and herself so that it showed only her sister, then texted it to the others. Once that was done, she started writing the text for her post. Until recently, Katrina and Vance had posted to her social media accounts on her behalf, giving her words she never would have chosen. Now the words were all hers, and this post was more important than anything she'd ever done. It needed to make an emotional impact if she wanted people to take it seriously. And it had to be taken seriously, because it needed to go viral as quickly as possible. She carefully crafted a message explaining what had happened and pleading for help. She tried to convey how important her sister was to the family, and especially to her, and to express gratitude to those willing to search.

At the bottom she added hashtags: #BrennaVanderhaven #missingperson #findmysister #rallythetroops #pleasehelp #findBrenna #emergency #pleasepray #searchforBrenna #missingchild #lost #mustfind #missinghermorethananything.

Her mother was silent but fidgeting. She sighed sadly and stared up at the ceiling.

"What are you thinking?" Cece asked, glancing her way.

"I'm wondering where my baby could be. I just can't believe she's missing. We've always been so careful with you two. It's like she just slipped away." A tear slid down one cheek, and she wiped it away with a quick swipe of her fingers.

Cece reached over and patted her knee, then went right back to business. "Don't worry, Mom. It hasn't been that long. I'm sure we'll find her."

CHAPTER 12

*W*alking down the streets of Park Slope, Brenna was initially pleased with herself. Without any money, phone, or an adult by her side, she'd made her way to Brooklyn. Her mood sank when she realized she didn't know Nanny's address. She'd walked to Nanny's place from the subway many times, but she was always with Nanny, who knew the way, so she hadn't paid attention. She'd seen on the map that there was more than one Park Slope subway stop and had gotten off at the first one. Her thinking was that Park Slope was a neighborhood, and how big could a neighborhood be? If she walked enough, she was bound to find something that looked familiar.

The streets were lined with parked cars, but compared to where she lived, there was not nearly as much traffic. The sidewalks, too, were less crowded than in Manhattan. Trees lined the space between the sidewalk and the street, providing shade on this hot day. The street she was currently on featured a line of brick townhouses, each three stories tall. They looked similar to Nanny's and yet not quite right either. A set of concrete steps led up to each front door, just like Nanny's, but none of the doors were the dark-blue color she remembered. She also recalled flowerpots on either side of Nanny's door. Several of these homes had flowerpots, but none of them matched what she remembered.

Brenna kept walking, sure she'd find it.

She walked for what seemed like forever, hours maybe, but it was hard to say exactly how long it had been without her phone or a clock. It had to be close to dinnertime by now. Her legs were getting tired. She leaned against a wrought-iron fence, thinking things through. She knew Nanny's first name was Margaret, but she didn't know her last name. Her biggest problem was that she couldn't remember the address. Also, Park Slope had turned out to be bigger than she'd realized. Part of her wanted to give up, but she knew it would be better to have Nanny accompany her on the return home. If she came back by herself, her parents would be furious. Nanny had a way of smoothing things over, which would be helpful at a time like this.

No, she couldn't give up just yet. She'd go a few more blocks, and if that didn't lead her to the right house, she'd turn around and go back home.

She plodded on, seeking out the shade when she had a choice. Her feet were getting heavier, and her shirt stuck to her back. She wondered if her mother had noticed her absence yet. Most likely not, she thought. Sometimes she went hours without anyone checking on her. Once one of the maids had flipped on the light switch in her bedroom early one Saturday morning, waking her from a deep sleep, then bustled in with the vacuum cleaner. She'd already started vacuuming the rug when she noticed Brenna watching her from under her covers. The young woman had apologized, saying, "I didn't know anyone was in here. I'll come back later." It made Brenna feel like she was in the way.

There were times when both her parents were home busy

with their own activities and the whole day would pass with neither one of them spending even a single minute with her. She wouldn't see them until bedtime and then only to have them say good night.

More than anything, she wished they'd be more like Nanny, who was interested in what she had to say and laughed when Brenna acted silly. She exhaled sadly. Nothing came of wishing. Nanny said you couldn't change people. You could hope for change, of course, but the best thing to do was to work on yourself. She'd say, "If you're a complete person, it will bother you less when people are disappointing." Brenna could grasp what she was saying, but still she wished her parents could be different.

Continuing on down the street, she became aware of heavy footsteps coming up fast behind her. She slowed and moved to one side to let the person pass, and when he did, she noticed it was the creepy man from the subway. The one with the stubbly face, chapped lips, and coffee breath. He turned slightly and stopped. "Hey, I know you," he said, a grin coming slowly across his face. "We talked on the subway, remember? What a coincidence! Do you live around here?"

Even though his tone was friendly, she was on high alert. She doubted that they'd crossed paths by accident. How likely was that to happen? Brenna remembered the woman on the subway and how she'd pointedly addressed him, calling him a perv. A moment later she'd advised Brenna to move if someone was bothering her. *Don't give him that power.* She froze, considering her options. He was blocking the direction she was headed. If she turned and ran, would he follow her?

He folded his arms and smiled, waiting her out. She hadn't gotten a good look at him on the subway, but now she took note of his lanky frame and ill-fitting clothing: faded tan pants and a button-down shirt, wrinkled and untucked. The backpack he had slung over one shoulder was a dark-blue fabric, with several zippers across the top. He said, "I live right around the corner. We can walk together."

Once again, Brenna recalled the words of the helpful woman on the subway. *Don't give him that power.* She squared her shoulders. "No. Leave me alone."

His mouth twisted as if he was amused. "Aw, don't be like that. I'm not scary. I've got a niece about your age, remember? I'm trying to be helpful. I'd be glad to walk with you to get you where you need to be. Unless you're lost? Are you lost? If you are, we can go to my house and you can call home."

"I'm not lost!" The words came out in a shout. Down at the end of the block, a woman was holding a watering can over a planter filled with brightly colored blooms. She paused to look in their direction. Brenna raised her voice again and said, "Leave me alone."

Brenna turned around and took off running, her legs pumping as fast as she was able. She half expected him to follow her. She could imagine the feel of him grabbing the back of her shirt in an attempt to manhandle her, dragging her somewhere she didn't want to be. If he tried it, she had a plan. She was going to run up the steps of the nearest townhouse and bang on the door, asking for help. She'd scream at the top of her lungs if she had to. There was no way she'd go anywhere with him.

She turned at the corner, allowing herself to look behind her, but he hadn't followed. Instead, he'd continued on in the same direction; she could see his back receding in the distance. She began to have second thoughts. Maybe he wasn't a bad guy after all. Maybe he was someone's father, just heading home. Still, it hadn't felt right, and she was proud of how she'd handled it. It would be such a good story to tell Nanny when she finally arrived at her house.

She walked a few more blocks, turning occasionally at corners to throw the creepy man off her trail. Just in case. She'd denied being lost, but now she had to admit it to herself. She had no idea where Nanny lived, or even if she was close. Going by her own instincts, she felt as if she must be close, which was puzzling, because why hadn't she come across her place yet? Was it possible she'd not been paying attention and missed it? Entirely possible, she realized. And now she was thirsty and her legs felt wibble-wobbly. All she wanted was to find Nanny's house and get a cold drink and be wrapped in her loving arms. That was all she wanted.

She was hot and tired and lost. This whole thing had gotten so messed up.

Trudging onward, she decided to go just a few more blocks. If she still hadn't found Nanny's house, she would start looking for the subway station.

She had crossed the street when she heard his voice. "Hey!" he yelled. "Brenna?"

At the sound of her name, she turned. It was the creepy man, holding up a phone and taking her picture. "You're Brenna Vanderhaven, right? You need to come with me."

How did he find her again, and worse yet, how did he know her name? She'd been warned against strangers pretending to know her or saying that her parents had arranged for her to go with them. She knew this wasn't right.

He put down the phone and began walking toward her. Brenna swallowed the fear rising in her throat and took off running. She had been at least a block ahead of him. With any luck, she could outrun him and find help. Behind her, he continued calling her name.

Brenna ran faster than she ever had before, crossing the street and then crossing back again in the middle of the road to throw him off her trail. When she reached a stretch of town-houses with a low wall along the sidewalk, she hopped over to the other side and hid behind it, wedged between two small bushes. Sitting with her back against the wall, she was out of view of both the sidewalk and the street.

"Brenna?" She took note of his location by the sound of his voice, yelling as he searched for her. "Brenna Vanderhaven! You don't need to be afraid. I want to help you."

Brenna crouched down, making herself as small as possible. She heard his voice receding in the distance, but she didn't climb out of her hiding spot until she hadn't heard his voice for a long time.

She got out of her hiding spot and continued on, trying to figure out the way to the subway. She turned left at the next corner. Down the block she noticed a cluster of people lingering in front of one of the townhouses. As she got closer, she realized many of them were very young children, several holding the hand of an adult. The adults carried brightly colored wrapped presents topped with large bows. One little boy hopped alongside his mother. A shiny helium balloon had been attached to the wrought-iron railing leading up to the front door. The text on the balloon said "Happy First Birthday!" above an illustration of a birthday cake with one candle. One of the little girls wore diamond-patterned leggings, along with a flouncy gold-colored tunic top and a headband to match. It put Brenna in mind of the cutesy outfits her mother used to buy for her before Brenna started to have her own opinions about such things. Her mother had loved to accessorize every outfit, a talent that eluded Brenna, who couldn't understand why it mattered.

She paused as she approached, watching the excitement of the birthday party guests heading up the steps and into the townhouse. She remembered all of her own birthday parties and those she'd attended. The games, the gifts, the refreshments! The joy of knowing you were now one year older and would be able to have more privileges, like a bigger allowance and a later bedtime. Oh, to be a little kid again and have so much to look forward to. Not a care in the world.

Those were the days.

Brenna thought about the refreshments inside. At the very

least, there would be cake with frosting, ice cream, and soft drinks, maybe punch. If they were serving a meal, it would be kid friendly. Mac and cheese. Hot dogs. Pizza. At one of her parties, her mother had arranged for the caterers to set up a melted chocolate fountain. Guests used skewers to coat the fruit or candy of their choice. Cece had loved the chocolate-covered strawberries. Brenna's personal favorite had been chunks of marshmallow. Her mother was at her best when she was organizing big events, and she tried to outdo herself with every birthday. So many good memories.

Brenna thought about all the food possibilities at this mystery child's first birthday party, and her stomach rumbled. Even a sip of cold water would be refreshing. She was starting to feel sweaty and gross.

She rested her backside against the stone wall lining the sidewalk, noticing when an SUV pulled into a parking space nearby. Out of the vehicle came a couple older than her sister but younger than her parents. Both the man and the woman wore an expression of steely resolve, as if determined to make it to the finish line. When they got closer, she noticed that the woman looked about to cry. The man guided her protectively, a well-placed hand on the small of her back. As they walked by, he said, "We'll drop off the gift, stay a few minutes, and slip out. Don't worry, Lauren. I'll think of a reason. I'll make it about me." The woman nodded. He leaned in and said, "We'll get through this."

As the couple headed up the stairs, Brenna heard the sound of someone tapping on glass. She looked up to see a little girl and next to her a dog jumping up against the second-story window of the party house. Both of them stared down. The girl, who looked to be about four or five, waved, and Brenna glanced behind her to see who she might be waving to, but no one else was left outside. She waved back, and the girl responded with a grin. Her little brown-and-white dog bounded happily against the glass, his perky ears pointed upward.

The girl beckoned for her to come inside, and Brenna furrowed her brow, confused. She mouthed the question, *Me?* and gestured from herself to the girl. The girl bobbed her head with an emphatic yes. She pointed to Brenna and to the front door, and with a waving motion, she gestured for Brenna to join her indoors. Then she put both her hands together in a silent prayer and mouthed what could only have been the word *Please?*

Brenna watched, not sure what to think. Did this girl think she was someone else? Someone she knew? This little girl's mother was not going to be happy if she knew her daughter was inviting strangers into their house. She shook her head, and when the girl frowned, Brenna motioned, with a point of her finger, that she was on her way somewhere. The balloon tied to the railing bobbed in the breeze.

While she stood there vacillating, she heard a man's voice. "Brenna? It's me, Gracie's uncle. Let's talk!"

She didn't see him, but he was close. Too close. Terror grew like a weight in her chest.

Without another moment's hesitation, she went up the stairs. Taped on the outside of the door was a sign that said "Let Yourself In." She took the sign at its word, opened the door, and went into the little girl's house, not worried anymore that she was trespassing at the party. If the grown-ups asked what she was doing there, she'd explain about the creepy man and that the girl had gestured for her to come inside. If all went well, they'd know where Nanny lived and walk her to the house where she would be safe.

Stepping into the entryway, Brenna found herself alone, standing on a floral-patterned rug. The air indoors was a lot cooler than outside in the hot sun. She heard the chatter of party guests and the shrieks of tiny children coming from the living room down the hall. To her left a narrow staircase rose up at a sharp incline, and at the top of the stairs stood the little girl with the dog next to her. "Hello," Brenna said, rooted to the spot. Someone's mother was bound to come along and notice a strange child in the house, and if that happened, she thought it would be better just to stand right inside the door. She didn't want to push her luck.

"Come up by me!" the little girl said, beckoning again.

Brenna hesitated. This child must think she was someone she knew. She went to the base of the stairs and took a step up. "I don't know you," she called up to her. "I was just walking by."

"I know. It's okay that you don't know me."

"It's okay that I'm here? Because I feel kind of weird about it. Maybe I should check with your mom?"

"Don't talk to my mom. It's okay that you're here." The child put her hands together. "Please come up by me. Please? Just for a few minutes?"

Brenna reluctantly headed up the stairs, sneaking a look over her shoulder as she reached the top. The dog danced, its tail wagging, and the girl looked just as happy. She said, "I was so happy you saw me and came in."

"I wasn't sure I should. Aren't you having a birthday party?"

"No, that's not for me. It's for my little brother. He turns one today." The girl was walking down the hall as she talked, the dog at her heels. "Let's go in my room."

She turned and went down a hall leading to the front of the house and went into a bedroom done in pink and white. Off to the right, a dresser against the far wall was topped by a framed photo of the little girl at the beach with a woman standing behind her, her hands resting on her shoulders.

In the center of the room was a canopy bed with sheer bed-curtains tied back on each post. Twinkle lights were strung across the top. On the floor sat an ornate dollhouse, and in the corner built-in shelving held toys, most of them stuffed animals and dolls. "Oh, this is pretty," Brenna said. "I like your room. Mine can get kind of messy."

"It always looks this way," the little girl said.

"Then you must not be as messy as me. My nanny says my room always looks like a hurricane came through." Brenna walked over to the window and looked down at the street. No sign of the creepy man. Her panic was lessening. She stepped away from the glass, reminding herself that she was safe now.

The little girl said, "My mom likes my room to stay neat."

Brenna nodded. "Mine does too, but it hardly ever is clean. My name is Brenna."

The girl stood next to the bed, one hand resting on the comforter. She lifted up her hand to display four fingers. "I'm four, almost five, and I'm Summer."

"Your name is Summer?"

She nodded emphatically. "Because it's my mom's favorite season." She pointed at the dog. "His name is Baxter, just because. He's a rescue. He likes everyone in my family, but he loves me best."

"I would love to have a dog," Brenna said. "Baxter is cute." Hearing his name, Baxter nudged her hand with his nose until she started to pet him, and then he quivered with happiness, his tail wagging. Brenna looked at his dark chocolate eyes and proud, pointed ears and thought Baxter was just about perfect.

"So how come you aren't at the party?"

Summer shrugged. "It's not for me. It's for Oliver."

"But still, you should be there. He's your brother."

Summer fidgeted but didn't answer, making Brenna think that staying upstairs must be some kind of punishment. Finally, Brenna said, "Do you think your mom will mind if I use your bathroom?"

Summer shook her head and pointed down the hall. "That way."

In short order, Brenna had used the bathroom, washed her

hands, and had a drink of water from the faucet. She felt better already. When she got back to Summer's bedroom, the girl was standing at the window looking down. Brenna joined her, watching a couple come out of the house and head to their car. Brenna recognized them as the man and woman who'd arrived after the rest of the guests, the man saying he'd make an excuse for them to leave early. "That's my aunt and uncle," Summer said, her forehead against the glass. "My uncle Scott and aunt Lauren. She's my mom's sister."

"She's pretty."

"She is pretty and nice too. She didn't want to come today. She thinks my mom is mad at her."

"Is she?"

"No." Summer shook her head. "Not anymore. My mom said some things that hurt my aunt's feelings. She didn't mean to. She was just upset."

"Your mom should tell her she's sorry."

"I guess."

"It's simple to say you're sorry."

"They just don't talk anymore. Both of them are sad." Summer went on, telling her how her aunt used to babysit for her, and chattering endlessly about the new baby girl cousin who would be arriving in the wintertime.

Brenna didn't want to interrupt her, but she really had to. She waited until Summer took a pause and then quickly spoke up. "I need to talk to your mom," Brenna said. "I'm trying to find my nanny's house. She lives in Park Slope in a house with a dark-blue door. She has flowerpots on her porch, and her first name is Margaret. Do you know someone like that?"

Summer pursed her lips, deep in thought, and then finally said, "No."

"Would you come downstairs with me so I can ask your mom or dad? If they don't know where Nanny lives, maybe they'd let me use their phone so I could call my sister." Calling

Cece was a good idea. Although on second thought, Brenna didn't have Cece's number memorized. In her phone, Cece was just listed in the contacts.

"You better not go down right now," Summer said. "My mom and dad won't like it. It will spoil Oliver's party."

"I wouldn't spoil it. I would just ask."

"You better wait. At least until after they open gifts."

"I can wait a little bit," Brenna said. "But not too long. My mom and dad are going to notice I'm gone at bedtime. That's when they usually come to look for me."

"The party won't last that long. My mom says Oliver has a short attention span."

Summer climbed up on the bed and patted the space next to her until Baxter jumped up to join her. Brenna sat on the opposite side, petting Baxter in a slow rhythm. She felt her hand get heavier and her eyelids drooping. The long walk in the heat was taking its toll, and she began to feel drowsy. "Maybe I'll just rest a bit," she said. "If you don't mind."

"I don't mind," Summer said.

CHAPTER 13

*S*cott held the car door open for Lauren. Five years married and he still treated her the same as when they were dating. Every day he had a compliment for her, and it was never of the cheesy scripted variety. He marveled at her generous spirit and her knack for improvisational seasoning in the kitchen. At the theater he still liked to put his arm around her shoulders, making two become one. Her friends were jealous of how attentive he was. *A husband who listens! A man who admits when he's wrong!* they'd say in mock awe. He always said he was lucky to have found her, but she felt like the lucky one.

When he climbed into the driver's seat, he glanced her way and said, "It's a long drive from South Orange for a twenty-minute stay." He set his phone on the console between them. "It's not even five-thirty yet."

"You said you didn't mind." She fastened her seat belt with a firm click.

"I didn't mind either way. It just seemed like Callie wanted us to stay longer. She said she was glad you were there."

"She was being nice." Lauren had seen the pain in Callie's

eyes; her sister could barely stand to look at her. Going to the party had been a mistake. Her continued presence could only ruin it.

Scott meant well. He was all about repairing relationships. The rift between Lauren and Callie wasn't a disagreement. There was nothing to repair. No apologies that could be said to fix things between them. The only thing that could help would be for Lauren to go back in time and do things differently. A whole-day do-over. She'd do it if she could, even if it meant giving up her own life in the process. It had been the worst day imaginable, and even mired in her own guilt and shame, she knew her sister felt a thousand times worse.

"Oliver seemed pretty excited," Scott said, starting the engine. "And the cake was cute."

"The cake was adorable," she admitted. Callie had outdone herself, baking the sheet cake herself and decorating it with a plastic train. The train went around on plastic tracks, circling the words *Happy Birthday, Oliver.* Thinking about it reminded her of her sister's creativity in making Summer's first birthday cake: a Barbie doll set right in the middle of a Bundt cake. The cake itself had been carved and frosted to resemble a ball gown. It was so beautiful. All the guests had admired it, saying that Callie could open her own custom cake bakery.

Callie. Thinking about those days tore at her. They'd once shared everything, but now it was as if the magnets of their friendship had been flipped. No matter how much she wanted to be close again, there was a force keeping them apart. Lauren opened the glove compartment and pulled out a wad of tissues and silently wept into one of them.

"Someday the two of you will have to sit down and talk," Scott said, his voice kind. "You can't go on like this."

"I know," she said, sniffling. "But not today." Not on Oliver's birthday, and not with all those people there, neighbors and friends and other relatives. All of them had to know what had happened. Did they judge her? They must. Three years had elapsed, and people talked. Everyone must know that her sister and her husband's unimaginable suffering was all her fault.

She needed to forgive herself, but she couldn't even imagine where to begin.

CHAPTER 14

*U*sing his phone, Dalton navigated from the subway stop to Nanny's townhouse. It looked very much like the others on the block. The main thing setting it apart was the dark-blue door and the flowerpots on either side of the stoop. To Greta, used to Wisconsin suburbia, the whole row of townhouses looked like a movie set. "Pretty nice neighborhood for someone who works as a nanny," Dalton said, a note of approval in his voice.

"Nannies shouldn't have nice homes?" Greta let go of his hand as they approached the stairs.

"Nannies should definitely have nice homes," he said. "It's just that most of them couldn't afford this neighborhood." He gestured down the block. "Most of these places would sell for at least two million."

"Two million *dollars?*" Greta was aghast. She looked up at the narrow three-story townhouse wedged in between the ones on either side of it. Even if it had a yard in back, the property couldn't be very large. "You could get a mansion in Wisconsin for two million dollars."

"True, but then you'd be in Wisconsin." He gave her a teasing grin.

"Hey!" She punched him in the arm. "Watch it."

"Sorry."

As they got to the top of the stairs, Greta remembered something. "Cece said Nanny lives with her nephew and his wife. They travel a lot, and she keeps an eye on things while they're gone. I assumed they lived with her, but it's probably the other way around."

"Most likely." He knocked on the door, and then they waited. And waited some more. He knocked again.

Greta found herself tapping her foot, anxious. Even though she enjoyed having time with Dalton, she hadn't lost sight of the fact that the reason they were venturing to Brooklyn right now was because Brenna, shy little Brenna, was missing. Every minute she wasn't found was another moment she could possibly be in danger. She thought about how quiet Brenna had been when Greta had first arrived in New York. The little girl had barely spoken a word and seemed unable to meet her gaze. That hadn't lasted long. Before she knew it, Brenna had opened up, especially when it was just the three of them: Cece, Brenna, and herself. The two sisters giggling together over something as silly as cat videos was contagious, and Greta found herself drawn into the circle. In a way, she got a glimpse of what it would be like to have a little sister herself, something she'd always wanted.

The police had mentioned that kids sometimes went to a friend's house without telling their parents, but Greta got the sense this was something bigger than that. Even as a kid back home in Wisconsin, she would always let her parents know when she headed out to visit someone. The Vanderhaven daughters lived in Manhattan and came from a prominent family. Brenna was the younger sister of a celebrity and was aware that her family was under constant scrutiny. It seemed unlikely that she'd take off on her own to visit a friend. She had to have been upset or influenced by someone else.

Dalton tried again, this time pounding on the door with the side of his fist. If someone was home, they'd have to hear it this time. Greta said, "I'll call her again." She pulled her phone out of her purse, checking for any texts before dialing Nanny's cell. She put it on speakerphone, so both of them heard it go to voice mail.

From the phone, Nanny's warm voice enveloped them: "You've reached Margaret Cragen. I'm not available right now. Leave a message. Thanks."

After the beep, Greta was just about to leave another message when the door opened abruptly, Nanny on the other side; she wore jeans and a loose-fitting top, and her hair was messily tucked behind her ears. Her eyes were bleary, but she managed a smile when she spotted Greta. Smoothing her hair back, she said, "Greta and Dalton! What a surprise."

"Sorry to barge in on you like this," Greta said.

"No, it's fine. I apologize for my appearance. I think I'm starting to get a bronchial thing." She gestured to her head.

"Ah, sorry to hear that." Dalton gave her a sympathetic nod.

"We tried calling but only got your voice mail," Greta said.

"I shut my phone off when I went to take a nap," Nanny said. "Why? What's wrong?"

Greta said, "We came to talk to you because Brenna is missing," at which point, Nanny's expression grew serious; her hand flew to her mouth. Wordlessly, she opened the door and let them in.

In the front entryway, Dalton said, "She's not here, by any chance? Have you heard from her?"

Nanny shook her head. "I haven't seen her since yesterday. I did get a voice mail from Mr. Vanderhaven saying I was fired, and then about half an hour later, Mrs. Vanderhaven called and

I answered. She said it was a misunderstanding and that not only was I not fired, but they were giving me a sizable bonus."

"That's so weird," Greta said, baffled. "Did she explain what happened?"

"No, and I didn't ask. Harry Vanderhaven is prone to making snap judgements and quick decisions. He's done this kind of thing before with other employees, so it wasn't a complete shock. Still, I was glad to hear I still had a job." She ushered them into a small living room, and Greta and Dalton sat down on a couch opposite an ornate fireplace. "So tell me about what happened with Brenna."

Greta said, "We think it started when Cece had a talk with her parents after they got back from their trip. She told them she was going to be taking charge of her own life and that she'd moved out and was living in Katrina and Vance's old apartment."

"That couldn't have gone well."

"Cece said it went better than she expected, actually."

"Were they arguing? Brenna doesn't like any kind of conflict. She even hates it when I speak more loudly than usual."

"No arguing that I heard of. Brenna was there during their talk, but Cece said she didn't seem upset. Her parents also brought her a gift from their trip, a stuffed dog she didn't like, and her father said she was being ungrateful."

"She's been wanting a dog, but I knew her parents would never go for it." Nanny clutched a tissue and leaned forward, listening intently. "Did she leave a note?"

"Not that anyone could find," Greta said, "All I know is that after Cece went back to our apartment, Brenna went to her room while her parents were talking. When they checked on her later, she was gone. The doorman said she left, saying she wanted to take a walk around the block."

"When was this?"

Greta looked to Dalton for confirmation. "Three hours ago, give or take?" He nodded. "So not that long."

"For her, that's a long time, though," Nanny said thoughtfully. "She's a homebody. Even when we go on outings she stays right by my side. Always has. When she was just a teeny, little girl, she would snake her hand up the sleeve of my sweater and grab hold of my elbow." She patted her elbow, remembering. "I can't imagine she'd just take off on her own. Were the police called?"

Dalton nodded. "They've issued a Missing Child Alert, and Cece is using her social media accounts and asking her followers to look for Brenna."

"And the police are looking at security cameras, I would imagine, and canvassing the area?"

Dalton said, "It sounds like they're doing everything they can."

"I wonder," Greta said thoughtfully, "if she left because she overheard her dad talk about firing you?" All three of them contemplated the idea silently. It made sense.

Finally, Dalton leaned forward, his elbows resting on his knees. "Could you check your phone and see if she left you any messages?"

Nanny stood up abruptly. "Let me go get it."

CHAPTER 15

*H*arry Vanderhaven was a man who took pride in being in charge. At the office he kept a tight schedule and prided himself on his quick and firm decision-making. It had been a long time since he'd found himself in a situation where he didn't know what to do, so today he felt completely shaken. He wandered out of the lobby of his apartment building, cell phone in hand. Cooper, the guy who'd let Brenna walk out the door, was no longer on duty, and the doorman who opened the door for him didn't greet him as cheerily as usual, but just murmured, "I hope your daughter is home soon."

Harry nodded. "Thank you."

Once out on the sidewalk, he viewed the street with new eyes. How would an eight-year-old girl see things? He had no clue. He tried to form a picture of his daughter in his mind but came up short. Her hair was about shoulder length, or maybe longer. As long as she had some say in the matter, Deborah always liked the girls' hair on the longer side, and Brenna was still young enough to fall into that category. What else did he know about her? Brown eyes, straight teeth, average height for her age, or so he thought. The last time he'd really taken notice of his younger daughter's height was when they'd posed for the family Christmas card, because she had been positioned next to him. Certainly she'd grown in the months since then, but he couldn't say for sure.

He backed up against the building and switched his attention to his phone, bringing up the picture of Brenna. He walked over to a bike messenger who'd stopped to adjust his helmet strap and tapped him on the shoulder. Holding the phone in front of him, he said, "My daughter is missing. Have you seen her, by any chance?"

The guy pursed his lips while studying the image, then shook his head. "Sorry, man. Once I start riding, I don't pay much attention to anything but my route. I got deadlines to meet."

"I understand. Thank you." Farther down the block, he approached two young women wearing business attire and interrupted their conversation, saying, "Excuse me, have you seen this little girl? She's eight years old and has been missing for a few hours."

They glanced down at the screen. "Sorry, no." The taller of the two clasped his arm. "Is this your daughter?"

"Yes." His voice came out hoarser than he'd intended. "Her name is Brenna."

"I'll say a prayer she comes home safely to you, and soon."

"I will too," her friend added, her voice laced with concern.

"I appreciate that. Thank you." He was surprised by how much their kind words affected him—like a jolt to the heart. They didn't know his family at all, but they'd offered him sympathy and prayers. He felt like some imaginary hand had soothed his forehead, like a mother comforting a feverish child. *I will get through this,* he thought. *We will get through this.* He imagined Brenna coming home and envisioned himself wrapping his arms around her.

He continued on. Fifteen minutes later, he encountered an old lady standing near the curb, rifling through a wheeled personal cart the size of a suitcase. "Excuse me," he said.

When she turned to him, he noticed her matted hair, disheveled clothing, and an odor suggesting she'd missed more than one day's shower. He would guess that she was homeless and the items in this cart her worldly possessions. "Yes?" When she smiled, he noticed a gap next to one of her front teeth.

"My daughter is missing," he said, showing her the phone. "Have you seen her? She's eight years old, and we don't know where she is."

The woman shook her head. "No, I'm sorry. I wish I could tell you different, but I haven't seen her."

"Thank you anyway."

Harry was halfway down the block when he heard the woman call out, "Sir, wait a minute!"

He stopped and turned to see her trotting down the sidewalk, one hand dragging the rattling cart behind her. When she caught up to him, she held out her closed hand. "I have something for you. It has helped me, and it might bring you some comfort." She dropped something into his palm.

There in his hand was a gold-colored coin with the image of an angel stamped on it. He'd never seen anything like it. Most likely it was a novelty item, certainly not real gold, but still, the gesture touched him. "I can't take this—"

"Rubbish," she said. "Something told me to give it to you, and so I did. You can't give it back."

"Well then, thank you." He flipped it over to see the same angel on the back. The picture was strangely comforting.

"It might help you find your little girl," she said. "I'll be keeping her in my prayers. What's her name?"

"Brenna."

"Brenna," she repeated. "What a lovely name. I hope you are

reunited soon and that your daughter knows how much you love her."

He watched as she walked away, stunned at her words.

And that your daughter knows how much you love her. A simple statement, but one that cut right to the heart, given his relationship with his children.

He'd prided himself on being a better father than his own father had been, but of course that hadn't taken much. His father had been both abusive and a drunk, while Harry was neither. His daughters had been spared from the horror of his own childhood. Even so, he knew he could have done better. He could have been more attentive, more demonstrative in his dealings with his daughters. It seemed to come naturally to other men. Why was it so hard for him to hug and kiss his own children? It felt awkward. He hadn't done it when they were little, and he thought it might come off as odd to just start doing it now that they were older.

His time, though, that would have been an easy thing to give. Deborah had been asking him to commit to family dinners since the day Cece was born. So many times he had intended to cut his hours and be home by six each evening, but it never seemed to work out. Of course, Deborah wasn't much better. Most of the time neither of them were home for dinner. At least the girls had each other. He knew other high-powered families who operated the same way, and their kids turned out fine.

Harry's biggest excuse the last few years was that things had been crazy at work, but then they'd always been crazy. Forward motion was how empires were built. There was always something that needed his immediate consideration. Some fire that needed to be put out, some emergency requiring his full attention. He was the only one who could attend to such things, while Brenna had her sister and Nanny and Deborah. He always felt that she was covered. He felt that he could give himself a good grade for providing well for his family, even as he knew his parenting style lacked the personal touch. He'd failed in that area.

He set off down the block, saying a silent prayer as he walked. *Dear God, just give me my daughter back, and I promise I'll become a better father and a better person.*

Please, just give me a chance to make it right.

CHAPTER 16

*C*ece had designated the formal living room of the Vanderhaven apartment as command central. On the coffee table in the living room she had two laptops and two tablets set up, each of them open to one of her social media accounts. She and her mother each had their cell phones set down within easy grabbing distance, in case the police, Harry, Greta, Dalton, or Nanny called.

When Roger called shortly after she'd posted online and asked if he could help, she'd told him to come right over, that they could use another set of hands to scroll through comments. This, she felt, was the key to ascertaining if anyone knew Brenna's whereabouts. Roger arrived in record time, greeting Cece with a hug and offering his sympathies to her mother. "I was so sorry to hear Brenna is missing, Mrs. Vanderhaven. I've gotten very fond of her in the short time since I've known Cece. When I think of that little girl out there all alone . . ." His gaze went to the window.

Cece saw her mother's lip tremble; she jumped in before he could say anything else. "It's only been a few hours, and she just went for a walk," she said brusquely. "Trust me, we're going to find her. She'll be back in no time." She pointed to a couch cushion. "Sit here."

Roger took a seat and adjusted his glasses on the bridge of his nose. "Yes, ma'am."

Only Cece knew that this show of confidence was a good front. She was as uncertain and afraid as her mother was, but it didn't do any good for both of them to get mired in negativity. Besides, she'd put out a call for all of Manhattan to watch for Brenna, and now she had a responsibility to follow through on the responses. So if she was being a little bossy, it was for good reason. Besides, after all the years of having her life orchestrated by others, it felt good to be in charge.

She handed Roger a tablet and told him what to look for. "Ignore the well-wishers and the haters. We don't have time to respond to comments or answer questions. Just scroll through and let me know if anyone has information about Brenna or says they saw her. My mom saw some disturbing stuff some sicko posted, so we'll probably come across more of that. Just ignore it." One account under the name Your_Biggest_Nightmare had posted a photo of roadkill with the caption, "Is this your sister?" Cece's mother had been so upset that she'd fled the room and didn't come back for fifteen minutes. When she'd returned, Cece had offered to let her off the hook. "Why don't you take a nap, Mom? Or a hot bath? I've got this."

"No," she'd said. "I want to help. I can't sit here and do nothing while Brenna is still missing."

Since then she'd sat quietly, scrolling through comments on Cece's Instagram account and periodically checking her phone to make sure she didn't miss any calls or texts. All three of them sat with their eyes fixed on a screen and one finger continuously poised. Swipe. Read. Swipe. Read.

Cece glanced over the comments, mentally thanking all of the followers who'd left nice messages. There were those who offered to hit the streets and look, as well as those who offered sympathy and prayers. Collectively, the positive comments outweighed the nasty ones by a lot. She let her eyes gloss over the ones who insinuated that her family deserved a disaster. That they'd skated by on their good looks and wealth for so long that they were due to know how the rest of the world lived. "Maybe this will make you appreciate what's important in life," one woman had written scornfully. As if Cece's whole life had been nothing but parties, rainbows, and unicorn rides. *You don't know me,* she thought. *You have no idea what my life is like.*

She took a deep breath and exhaled her stress, willing her tight shoulder muscles to relax. There was no good in carrying her anxiety around with her. None of that would help find Brenna.

Each of them concentrated on the task at hand, taking only short pauses to rub their eyes or shift position. At one point, Cece glanced up to see Roger looking her way. He gave her a slight smile that she knew was meant to be encouraging. Before she could smile back, he'd dropped his gaze back down to his screen.

One of the maids came with glasses of ice water topped with lemon slices. Each of them accepted a glass, murmuring their thanks before getting back to work.

Deborah spoke. "Someone thinks they saw Brenna in the East Village, and they took a picture of the girl." She turned the screen toward Cece. "There's no way that's Brenna. Right?" The photo was taken from behind, but even without seeing a face it was clear to Cece it wasn't her sister. This girl had the physical build of a teenager and was carrying a designer purse. The hair was the right color, but longer than Brenna's.

"Definitely not Brenna," Cece said. "Thank them and let them know it's not her."

"I didn't think it was her," her mother said, her voice disappointed. She turned back to the laptop and typed in a response. "I mean, it didn't look like her, but I wanted to be sure."

"Mom, I know it's a letdown, but it shows that people are looking. To me that means it's only a matter of time before someone spots her."

"You really think so?"

Cece nodded. "I'm sure of it."

When her mother's cell phone rang, all three of them froze. She picked it up with shaky hands. "Deborah Vanderhaven." A pause. "Yes, Detective Zagon? You have some news?" Cece studied her mother's face, hoping it would show that she was hearing positive news. She wished her mother would put it on speakerphone. Her mother nodded. "I understand. Thank you for letting me know." It was clear from her defeated expression that good news hadn't been shared. "Yes, of course. Please keep us updated."

After she'd clicked off, Cece said, "So?"

Her mother sighed. "There was nothing on the laptop that showed Brenna had been corresponding with anyone or participating in any message boards or group chats. She also hadn't looked up maps or googled anything unusual. There was nothing on there that made it look like she'd planned to run away."

Cece had already known that would be the outcome. Brenna was closely monitored, but even if that weren't the case, she wasn't a devious child. Even as a toddler and preschooler, she listened to the adults. There were no tantrums, no fits if she didn't get her way. She was, in a word, complacent. "I could have told them that."

"They're just doing their job." She reached over and placed the phone on the end table. "They also reviewed security cameras and traffic cams in the area. She did go in the direction the doorman said, and they were able to follow her for a few blocks and then they lost her. It was near a stairwell going down to the subway, so they're guessing that's where she went."

Roger hesitantly spoke up. "They have cameras in the subways, though. Can't they check them?"

Her mother nodded. "That's what they're doing next. He said it's very painstaking work. They don't want to rush the process and miss something." She cleared her throat. "He's going to keep us updated and said if we find out anything from your followers, we should notify them immediately."

Cece said, "Of course."

They continued on, the minutes turning to an hour and then to two. The silence was broken when Roger said, "This might be something." Cece glanced over to see his brow furrowing as he stared at the screen. A lock of hair flopped onto his forehead, resting on the rim of his glasses. His lips moved slightly as he read over something on the page.

"What?"

"This commenter, Robyn. She says her mother saw a little girl who looked exactly like Brenna on the subway this afternoon."

Cece felt a shiver go up her spine. "When?"

"She didn't give a time. She said the little girl told her she was going to visit her grandmother."

"Oh." Cece couldn't keep the disappointment out of her voice. One set of their grandparents were dead, and the other pair lived in Wisconsin. They barely knew the Wisconsin relatives, and she was certain Brenna didn't know where they lived. There was no way her sister would be going to visit them. "That's not her, then."

"She said the little girl got off at Park Slope in Brooklyn."

"That's where Nanny lives." Her mother looked up, suddenly alert. "In a brownstone in Park Slope with her nephew and his wife."

Roger kept reading. "The little girl mentioned her nana had two cats named Fanta and Smokey."

Cece felt her heart accelerate, and a bit of hope poked

through. "Those are the names of Nanny's cats. That was her. That was Brenna."

"I'll call Detective Thompson and let him know," her mother said. With shaking hands, she picked up her cell phone and pecked out the number on his business card. She held the phone up to her ear. "Yes, Detective Thompson? This is Deborah Vanderhaven. One of Cece's followers spotted Brenna on the F train heading into Brooklyn earlier today. Yes, we're sure it was her." She explained about the cats and that the woman thought she was visiting her nana, when most likely she misunderstood that Brenna was going to see her nanny.

As Cece watched, her mother seemed to gain her composure. "Yes, if you want." She turned to her daughter. "He's going to come back here to go over what you've found. If you want to contact that woman in the meantime, they're going to want to question her."

"I'm on it." Cece went to message Robyn, to let her know that the police wanted to ask her mother a few questions. She'd just finished typing in the words when Roger loudly cleared his throat. She looked his way. "What?"

Roger had a worried look in his eyes. "I hate to show this to you, but you have to see it." He handed her the tablet; he'd enlarged a message that was accompanied by a photo of Brenna, wearing today's clothing. In the picture she stood on a sidewalk in what could have been Brooklyn. Her body faced forward, and her head was turned back to look behind her. It was the look on her face, one of fear, that Cece found alarming. The message, from someone named CoolManLuke, said, "Hi Cece, I know where your sister is. In exchange for $5,000 cash, I will give you the information. Meet me at 7:00 p.m. sharp. Thanks." Below that was the name and address of a coffee shop in Brooklyn.

"Oh no. Please, no." Cece felt her throat constrict, leaving her lightheaded.

"What?" Her mother had just finished the conversation with the detective and set the phone down.

Wordlessly, Cece handed her mother the tablet, then watched her face as she read the message. "I'll call the detective back and tell him we have another update," she said smoothly.

To Cece, her mom seemed not to have a grasp on the enormity of this new development. Fifteen minutes ago her mother was a nervous wreck, and now suddenly she had her old air of assurance. Didn't she realize that someone had snatched Brenna and now wanted ransom money? Horrible scenarios ran through Cece's mind. Brenna in a locked room or the trunk of a car. Brenna alone and scared, crying for help. No, she couldn't think like that. It didn't help anything.

Her mother called the detective back and told him about the message, reading it out loud and describing the photo. "It's definitely Brenna," she said. "She looks worried, but it was taken at a distance, so it's hard to tell. Just a minute." She changed her focus to Cece. "Can you send him a screenshot?"

Cece nodded mutely and got to work.

"Okay, then. Keep us updated." She clicked off and set the phone on the coffee table.

"What did he say?" Cece asked. It would be so much easier if her mother would just put it on speakerphone. Someone needed to teach her Cell Phone 101.

"They're going to send someone to the coffee shop to pick up the guy, and then they'll question him. It sounds like they'll be able to charge him with something."

"Charge him with something? Don't you mean kidnapping?" Cece asked.

Her mother's blue eyes flickered with confusion, and then her expression changed with the realization of what Cece was saying. "Oh, honey, did you think the person who sent this message has Brenna?"

"Well, of course that's what I think. He sent the picture. It was taken today. And look." She pointed at the image on the tablet. "She looks afraid." She set the tablet down on the table, and Roger picked it up.

"Well, yes, she could be afraid. Or it could just be that she's startled or worried."

"How can you be so blasé about this?" Cece asked. "Brenna is missing, and this man may have her."

"Oh, honey." Her mom slid closer and put her arm around her shoulder. "I know this is scary, but just take a deep breath. This does not fit a kidnapping."

"How can you be so sure?" Out of the corner of her eye, Cece spotted Roger watching the two of them sympathetically.

"Your father and I have insurance covering abductions, and as part of it, we were tutored in how best to prevent our children from being kidnapped. The lessons also covered how it tends to work. Believe me, this message is not from an experienced criminal. It comes from an account that can be traced, and he set up the meeting in a public place. He mentions information, but not that he actually has Brenna. He asks for money, but doesn't say what will happen if he doesn't get the money. He didn't say specifically that you had to deliver the cash. And really, five thousand dollars? How insulting."

"Maybe because he's asking for cash, he made it a lower amount?"

"More likely he's some dimwitted opportunist looking for an easy payout."

"I don't know." Cece shook her head. "I'd like to believe that, but Brenna is still out there somewhere, and maybe this guy saw something. Maybe he saw someone else take her?" She took a deep breath.

"The police will pick him up, and we'll find out more. Until then, we really don't know anything." Her mother's voice was soothing, and Cece rested her head on her shoulder.

Roger held up his hand, like he was a schoolboy answering a question. "If I may?"

Cece lifted her head. "Yes?"

"I think your mom is onto something." He held up the tablet. "If you look at CoolManLuke's account, he has photos taken around the city, and a few of the pictures show some guys drinking at a bar. A few people left comments like they were there. If he *is* a criminal, he's not a very smart one."

"Maybe he's using someone else's account." Cece couldn't quite let go of her fear. "Or hacked into a stranger's account?"

"If he did that," Roger said, "he'll have left some kind of digital footprint. The police would be able to find him."

"We'll know soon enough," her mother said. "In the meantime, I'll call your dad to give him the update and you two keep looking at messages."

CHAPTER 17

Callie gently lowered a sleeping Oliver into his crib so as not to wake him. His eyelids fluttered as she slid her hands out from underneath him, and she held her breath, fearing a revival, but once his body was against the mattress, he settled in to sleep. She tucked a blanket around him and rearranged the stuffed animals at the end of the bed, putting his favorite one, a turtle he called Wummy, right next to him. She had a feeling he was down for the night, which was good because she and Colton were ready for a good night's sleep.

Oliver had been more tired than usual. He hadn't napped that day, probably because he'd sensed their frantic activity on the first floor as they'd been getting ready for the party. She'd put him in bed right after lunch, but she'd heard him over the monitor jabbering in his bed as she put the finishing touches on the cake and Colton blew up balloons. She'd already planned for a few easy party games for the children. For food she had plates of cut fresh fruit, individual bags of potato chips, and trays of small sandwiches. They'd deliberately kept the party simple. Oliver was only turning one and wouldn't know the difference. Once he was older, they'd have to up their game, but at this point he was happy with new toys and being the center of attention.

The party was a success, with the exception of the barely there attendance of her sister, Lauren, and brother-in-law, Scott. They'd shown up on time with a lovely wrapped gift, then stayed for less than half an hour before bolting out of there. Scott had used his IBS as an excuse, which was likely to be true, but she still found it annoying. If he hadn't felt well, he could have stayed at home and Lauren could have come alone. It's not like Oliver would have known. Their leaving so quickly was exceptionally aggravating because she'd changed the party from an afternoon event to five o'clock solely for their convenience, even though the timing wasn't ideal for the other guests. Parents of small children never wanted their kids to get riled up before bedtime. But because she didn't want to leave Lauren and Scott out, she'd rearranged the entire thing, making phone calls after the invitations had gone out because Lauren had begged off, saying that early afternoon wasn't good for them. All that trouble, and then they came and left as if they'd spotted a quarantine sign on the front door. It was like Lauren wasn't even trying to heal the rift between them. Granted, they'd gone through a difficult time, one she didn't even like to think about, but that was ages ago, and she felt terrible about it. She'd apologized and had tried so hard to repair their relationship, but Lauren wasn't making it easy.

Out in the hallway, she whispered, "Baxter?" and waited. A second later, she heard the plop of Baxter jumping off Summer's bed onto the rug and the jangle of his tags as he came to join her. She glanced at the darkened open doorway leading into her daughter's room and considered going in, then sighed and thought better of it. Better to leave things be. She reached down to pat Baxter. Such a good boy.

Silently, she went down the stairs with the dog at her side. It amazed her that he knew to be quiet while the baby slept. The dog had been a rescue, one of several puppies found in a box by the side of a highway in New Jersey. Who would do such a horrible thing? It was something she'd wondered a thousand times. With all the comfort Baxter had brought to her family, he was priceless and irreplaceable. Knowing that someone tried to throw him away like garbage made her teary every time she thought about it.

She let Baxter out the back door to do his business, and when he came back inside, she went to the pantry to get him a treat. He'd been such a trouper, staying upstairs during the party. One of the little girls was terrified of dogs, even small, well-behaved dogs, so Callie had taken him up prior to the guests' arrival and ordered him to stay. He was such a good dog. Baxter loved children. It had to have killed him to hear their voices on the first floor, but he was obedient and didn't venture down the stairs. She knew he wouldn't. "Yes, you are a good dog," she cooed, giving him a pet on the head and scratching behind his ears before going into the kitchen.

Colton had done all of the post-party cleanup while she had gotten Oliver in his pajamas and rocked him to sleep. Now the kitchen counters were spotless, and the leftover sandwiches and cake were wrapped and in the fridge. Colton sat on a barstool at the island, his attention locked on his tablet.

"He's completely out," Callie said, giving him the bedtime update. "I think it's going to be a quiet night." She was due for an uninterrupted night's sleep. Knowing her son was unlikely to wake during the night made her feel like this would be a good night to take an extra melatonin and surrender to sleep. Hopefully she'd get caught up and feel rested for once.

Colton met her eyes. "You know that Cece Vanderhaven you always talk about? Her sister is missing." He turned the screen toward her, displaying a photo of Cece with a little brown-haired girl.

Callie leaned in to take a look. "Brenna, right?" She'd been

89

following Cece's Instagram account for a while. Brenna wasn't included very often, but Callie was a pretty avid fan and knew as much as anyone did about the Vanderhaven family. Sometimes realizing how much time she wasted following the life of the privileged, she felt foolish, but she justified it as a being a guilty pleasure. Some people had martinis and chocolate. She had Cece Vanderhaven. It was fun to imagine living like those who were rich and famous. She and her sister, Lauren, used to talk about Cece as if they knew her. She missed those conversations. "I didn't know you followed Cece."

"I don't. There was an article on CNN, and I clicked on the link."

"Was she abducted?"

"No. It says here she was last seen leaving the family's apartment building on foot. She told a doorman she was going for a walk, but that was hours ago." He read the post aloud, ending with all the hashtags: #BrennaVanderhaven #missingperson #findmysister #rallythetroops #pleasehelp #findBrenna #emergency #pleasepray #searchforBrenna #missingchild #lost #mustfind #missinghermorethananything.

"Please pray?" Callie repeated. In all the years she'd followed Cece's account, she'd never heard a mention of anything faith related. Fashion, yes. High society events, of course. Hijinks featuring Cece and her friends Katrina and Vance? That was a given. But prayer? That was a new one. Callie knew a lot about prayer. She'd done more than her share, but it never seemed to help. Prayer, she'd decided, was what people did to keep themselves busy during crises. Like pushing the crosswalk button, it deluded them into thinking they had some control over the outcome. "I hope they find her," she said sincerely. Cece and her poor parents had to be going out of their minds with worry. She wouldn't wish that on anyone.

"I'm sure they will," Colton said. "It sounds like half of New York is looking for her."

CHAPTER 18

*L*uke Walters stood in front of the coffee shop, his backpack dangling from his fingertips. He hoped that Cece Vanderhaven herself would show up. Wouldn't that be a kick? If he got a selfie with her, he could show it to his ex-wife, Kelly, and that would definitely get her attention. *Loser*, she'd called him the last time they'd talked. *Dumbass* was another insulting word she'd aimed his way. Just because he'd lost another job. It wasn't his fault this time, not that she cared. He'd had an audition that couldn't be missed, a character on his favorite show, *Law & Order: SVU*. He'd called his manager at the restaurant to say he needed to get the morning off, but that guy didn't give a rat's ass. Fred had no soul. The man wouldn't budge, not even one little inch, which really sucked. Luke had covered for the other cooks plenty of times. You'd think they could do the same for him in return.

Well, he'd missed work and gone to the audition anyway, and he was glad he did. He'd nailed it, totally got the grit and substance of the character and impressed the casting director and his assistant. When he left, the casting director had said,

"We'll be in touch," and that's when he got the feeling he would be getting a callback.

Running into Brenna Vanderhaven that day was a stroke of luck. Kelly had a major girl-crush on Cece, and over the years she'd shown him videos from Cece's YouTube channel and talked nonstop about the Vanderhaven family. It had been a huge annoyance, although at the time he'd pretended to be interested, because when Kelly was happy the world was one big sunshiny place, and when she wasn't, well, a person quickly found out that even being in the same room with her was unbearable. He could be in the best mood and forget one little thing like picking up something at the store on his way home and she'd get that look on her face, the one that reminded him of storm clouds rolling in overhead just ready to burst. When that happened, he might as well kiss his happiness goodbye. Talk about a joy-killer. Still, he wanted her back in his life—or more precisely, he wanted her to want him back. To realize what she was missing without him.

This could turn out to be his lucky week, when everything changed for him. If all went well, he'd get the part on *Law & Order: SVU*, meet the famous Cece Vanderhaven, and come out ahead a cool five grand. Not a bad week's work. Kelly was going to be sorry she'd kicked him to the curb.

He hadn't recognized Brenna right from the start. He just knew she looked familiar. Honestly, he'd wondered if she was a child actor, someone he'd have seen in commercials or on the stage. She didn't really have the look, but something about her face nagged at him. When he finally figured it out, he did a quick search on his phone and confirmed it. And then when the news hit that Brenna Vanderhaven was missing, he knew he'd stumbled onto a gold mine. The Vanderhavens were billionaires. There's no way they'd miss a chance to exchange money for some information. To them, $5,000 was nothing. He thought of all the times he'd seen wealthy families in the news offering rewards for missing family members and knew the amount was always at least five figures. He purposely kept his request on the low side because he was a reasonable person.

He wasn't trying to bleed them dry. Just asking for his fair share.

Luke rested his back against the brick wall, peering down the block. He wondered if Cece or whoever came to meet him would arrive in a limo. He hoped so. It would be cool if they offered him a ride home. He'd have them drive him to his ex's place and text her ahead of time to give her advance notice. It wouldn't do any good if she wasn't looking out the window when they pulled up.

If it wasn't Cece, that would be a disappointment, but as long as the money was there, he'd keep up his end of the bargain. He'd tell them everything he knew, even lead them to the last place he saw her. They should be able to go from there. The Vanderhavens were so rich they could send an army with those new goggles he'd read about, the ones that combined night vision and thermal imagery. He was pretty sure those goggles could see into buildings too. They'd find that kid like nothing flat, and he'd be the one responsible. They might not want to give him credit. The authorities almost never gave hero citizens their due, but that would be okay. He'd know what he'd done.

He was still daydreaming about night vision goggles when a police car screeched to a halt in front of the coffee shop. Scared the hell out of him. When the door flew open, both officers jumped out with their weapons drawn. *What the what?*

Had something happened in the coffee shop while he was waiting? A holdup maybe? Luke dropped the backpack and stepped aside to give them access to the door, but now they were yelling at him.

"CoolManLuke? Are you CoolManLuke?"

"Yeah. What's going on?"

"Did you send a message to Cece Vanderhaven?"

He nodded mutely, looking back and forth between the two men in uniform, not computing what was happening. In a flash, one officer turned him around and slammed him face-first against the wall, slapping handcuffs on his wrists. Stunned, he shouted, "Why are you doing this? What's happening?"

The cop turned him around, pressing him against the side of the building while the other one went through his backpack. Luckily, he didn't have any drugs with him today, just a bottle of Jack Daniel's and a few scripts. He'd been practicing a monologue for film class. The beefy officer pulled his wallet out of the inside zippered pocket and looked through it, finally saying, "Is this you? Luke Walters?"

"Yes, that's my name, but what is this about?"

"Luke Walters, you are under arrest."

"For what?" Luke was indignant. He'd done nothing wrong. Anyone could send a message online, and anyone who didn't like the message could delete it. There were no laws on the internet. This couldn't be right.

"For kidnapping and extortion. You have the right to remain silent . . ."

As they shoved him into the car, making sure to push his head down as he went in, all Luke could think was that the only way this could suck more was if he didn't get the part on *Law & Order: SVU* after all.

CHAPTER 19

$\mathscr{L}$uke sat at the table, head in his hands, all alone. It had to be eighty degrees in the room, and the air was stagnant with humidity. He'd turned down a cup of water, recognizing it as a trick to get his DNA, but now, with beads of perspiration forming on his forehead, he wished he'd accepted the water after all.

They'd taken his backpack and his phone right at the start. Without them, he felt stripped bare.

This interrogation room was nothing like he'd seen on TV. True, it had the obligatory mirror that he knew was reflective only on his side, the other being a window for watching perps. Real perps, not innocent guys like him. The room, though, was smaller and so was the table, which was near the wall rather than in the middle of the room. After they'd led him in here, they'd instructed him to sit in the chair closest to the wall, and then the whole awful experience had begun—the two male detectives accusing him of horrible things, and him denying every single one of them in response.

They might have thought they were questioning him, but it seemed more like badgering, the way they twisted his words, trying to get him to admit that he'd done something wrong. The younger detective seemed to have a slightly softer edge to his words, but both of them acted as if he were clearly guilty. Luke was proud of how he'd held his ground, insisting that he hadn't so much as touched Brenna Vanderhaven and certainly wasn't trying to extort money from her family. "I was offering a simple trade," he'd said. "Information for money. You guys do that all the time, right? With informants? I'm like you."

Even as all this was happening, he tried to stay present, making mental notes of his emotional state and how it felt to be in this space. He sensed a push and pull between himself and the detectives and memorized the feeling for future use in his acting. *This will all get cleared up,* he thought, taking steady breaths to calm himself when he felt his heart racing. Once it was over, he knew he could use this experience. For him, having a firsthand experience was gold.

They had him go over the timeline multiple times, and yes, it sounded bad when he admitted tailing Brenna Vanderhaven in Park Slope, but he emphasized that he was doing it from a respectable distance and only because he wanted to help her.

"I have a niece her age. Her name is Gracie," he said. "I'd never hurt a child. You can ask anyone." He started to cry, more from frustration than anything, but he was able to look away and blink back the tears. They didn't even notice.

The two detectives had finally left the room after two hours of questioning him, and now here he sat, wondering if someone was watching him or if he was being filmed. When the door finally opened, it was the older man, the one who'd looked at him with contempt during questioning.

Luke lifted his head and met his gaze. "So?"

The detective cleared his throat. "You're being charged with harassment in the second degree and will be given a ticket to appear in court."

"Harassment? I didn't harass anyone," Luke said, indignant.

"You admitted to following Brenna Vanderhaven in a public place, right?"

Luke scoffed. "She barely knew I was there. And I was keeping an eye out for her more than anything." They should be applauding him for his efforts instead of running him down like this. Most people would have seen her and just gone about their business, not even caring.

"Tell it to the judge."

And that was it. After he collected his desk appearance ticket and retrieved his belongings, they said he was free to go. On the way out, he passed the younger detective, who stood with a paper cup in his hand. Luke stopped, unable to resist getting in the last word. "I told you I didn't do anything wrong," he said.

"Some friendly advice," the detective said, his tone not the least bit friendly. "You steer clear of Brenna Vanderhaven and her family. If we get any complaints, you better believe you're not going to be so lucky next time. I'll lock you up myself."

CHAPTER 20

$\mathcal{D}$ etectives Zagon and Thompson came back to the Vanderhaven apartment to follow up on both of the social media messages. Deborah had hoped to ask them about CoolManLuke right away, but the first order of business became questioning the elderly lady who'd spoken to Brenna on the subway. The woman's name was Gilda Gracia, and she came to the apartment accompanied by her daughter, Robyn, and granddaughter, Delia.

The detectives had offered to come to Gilda in order to question her, but she had insisted that she and her daughter and granddaughter were already in the city, right around the corner from the Vanderhavens, coincidentally enough. They offered to meet up at the Vanderhaven apartment, and Deborah had agreed.

Deborah found it awfully convenient that all three of them happened to be in the neighborhood when Cece answered their message. Especially odd that they'd be out so late at night with a child. She thought it was more likely that they'd orchestrated it that way in order to see their apartment and meet Cece in person. In a way, this wasn't surprising. So many people were curious about their life and home, especially since her older daughter had become famous. If it were up to Deborah, they'd have lived a more private life, but Harry had been raised by parents who relished showing their conspicuous wealth, and as a result, he thought nothing of allowing designers to lend Deborah expensive jewelry and clothing in exchange for her unspoken endorsement. The same was true of the interior designer who'd done their master bedroom and en suite bathroom update in exchange for name placement and photos in an online article. None of this seemed important today. She'd trade every inch of this apartment to get her daughter back.

The little girl, Delia, sitting on the couch next to her mother and grandmother, was close enough to Brenna's age to make Deborah want to cry. Cece and Roger now stood off to one side of the room, relinquishing their seats to the guests. Deborah swallowed the lump in her throat and forced herself to concentrate on what the detectives were asking.

"We didn't talk for very long," Gilda said, almost apologetically. "She just struck me as a very sweet, polite child." She looked straight at Deborah. "I could tell she was raised well."

"Thank you." Deborah tried to smile, but her lips wouldn't cooperate.

Detective Zagon said, "So you've already identified a photo of Brenna. I'm going to repeat what you just told me. If something is incorrect, or if you remember something else, let me know." He glanced down at his notes. "You were on the F train going to Brooklyn at about two p.m. and sat next to a child believed to be Brenna Vanderhaven. She told you she was going to visit her nana in Park Slope, and she talked about her nana's cats—Fanta and Smokey. You showed her pictures of your granddaughter, Delia, and your cat." He gestured to the little girl. "She got off on the Seventh Avenue stop, and that was the last you saw of her."

Gilda nodded. "That's exactly right."

"Was she carrying anything?"

"Like what?"

"A bag, a backpack, money, a phone?"

"No, I didn't see anything like that."

Gilda had a look of intense concentration, her mouth pressed together and her eyes narrowed. Her gray hair was pulled back, revealing large silver hoop earrings. Her purse was rattan weave, the kind sold at craft fairs. Her clothing was all cotton, solid colors. She reminded Deborah of an elderly hippie, the kind who might attend drum circles and refused to use anything plastic. Probably a vegan and a fanatic crusading to make the world a better place. But no, that was a mean thought. Deborah mentally shook the negativity out of her head, knowing that this woman really wanted to help, something that was endearing.

"Oh!" She raised one finger. "I just remembered something else. She also told me she wanted a dog more than anything, but her parents were opposed to the idea. I told her it was hard to have a dog in the city."

"It was definitely Brenna," Cece said, speaking up for the first time. "The Smokey and Fanta reference was spot-on, and no one else would know that. And the fact that she wants a dog is right too."

"She identified her by photo as well," Detective Zagon said.

Well, Deborah thought, the photo ID may have made it conclusive to him, but the fact that this woman knew the cats' names was far more convincing, in her opinion. People lied and for all kinds of reasons. Just being invited to their apartment would be enough of an incentive for someone to say they'd spotted Brenna. Of course, Gilda Gracia hadn't known they would invite her when she'd offered to speak to them and the police.

"I think we have enough information," Detective Thompson

said. "We've already shifted our search efforts to include that part of Brooklyn."

"Did you get anything else from the traffic cams?" Roger asked the detectives.

They shook their heads. Detective Zagon looked at Deborah and said, "We'll keep you apprised every step of the way. I have a daughter myself, and I know how worried I'd be if I wasn't sure where she was."

"Thank you." Deborah noted that he'd avoided using the word *missing*, something she appreciated. *Missing* meant there was a hole where Brenna should be. Saying they weren't sure where she was meant she was out there, waiting to be found.

"Do you have any other questions for Ms. Gracia?" Detective Thompson directed his question to the Vanderhavens.

"I do, actually," Deborah said. "How did Brenna seem? Was she upset?" Part of her hoped the answer would be yes. It would explain so much, but the older woman just shook her head.

"Honestly, she seemed fine. Not overly happy, but that's to be expected on the subway. She just seemed set on getting to her nana's."

They'd explained to her at the outset that there was no nana, that what Brenna had actually said was "Nanny," but this woman clearly didn't get it. Staring at her now, Deborah had such conflicting emotions. She was grateful that she'd taken the time to come forward, but infuriated that she hadn't done more while Brenna sat right next to her on the subway. "It didn't strike you as odd to see a young child all by herself leaving Manhattan?"

Gilda looked a little taken aback. "Well, no. I see kids riding the subway by themselves all the time."

Deborah gestured toward the woman's own granddaughter. "So you let Delia just come and go like that? Ride the subway without an adult?" Her tone came out more harshly than she'd intended.

KAREN MCQUESTION

The mother, Robyn, spoke up. "We don't let Delia ride by herself, but our family tends to be a bit overprotective. Lots of kids ride the subway on their own, though. It's not uncommon." She had her arm draped around her daughter's shoulders and protectively pulled her close.

"Mom, it's not her fault Brenna took off. She didn't know," Cece said diplomatically. "I have a question, Mrs. Gracia, if you don't mind."

"Of course. Anything to help." She shot a glance in Deborah's direction, and Deborah did her best to nod appreciatively.

Cece said, "Do you remember what Brenna was wearing?"

Mrs. Gracia's eyebrows knit together in thought. "Dark shorts, I think. And a solid-colored T-shirt—linen-colored, I'm pretty sure. I can't remember her footwear. Sandals, maybe?" She looked to Deborah. "Did I get it right?"

"Almost exactly. Pretty close," Deborah said, sadly realizing that this stranger remembered more details about her daughter's clothing than she herself had. She hadn't noticed what Brenna was wearing that day. Why hadn't she noticed? So much of the care of her household and children had been put on autopilot years ago. Her own mother had once told her that she led a selfish lifestyle. She'd been so insulted that the comment had caused her to pull away from her parents, but maybe her mother had been right. It wasn't that Deborah didn't care. It was that she didn't care as much as she should have. She hadn't put her daughters first, instead relegating the everyday decisions to Nanny and their teachers and their tutors. She'd deluded herself into thinking that since the girls were thriving, all was fine.

"I'm so glad." Mrs. Gracia clasped her hands together, as pleased as if she'd passed a test. "I've always been told I have a very good memory."

"Yes, you do." This time Deborah managed a halfhearted smile.

"I think we have everything we need," Detective Zagon said.

102

"Detective Thompson will escort you downstairs and make sure you get a cab ride home."

"We always take the subway," said the little girl.

"Oh no," Deborah said. "Ask the front desk to send a car around. Tell them it's for the Vanderhavens and that I personally requested it."

"That's so nice of you," Gilda said, standing.

"It's the least we can do." Deborah walked the group to the front door. "Thank you for all your help. We very much appreciate it."

Both mother and daughter answered.

"Good luck finding your daughter."

"We hope she's home soon."

When Deborah returned to the living room, she found Cece, Roger, and the detectives waiting for her. Detective Zagon said, "I have some news about CoolManLuke. Our guys picked him up in front of the coffee shop at seven right on the dot. They recognized him from the pictures online. His real name is Luke Walters. He admitted sending the message but was stunned to be arrested. Frankly, we don't think he knows anything. He said he realized who Brenna was, but she wouldn't talk to him. He followed her around for a bit in Park Slope. When she noticed him, she ran off and was able to lose him. Before that, he got the definite impression she was lost. She seemed to be looking at doorways, as if trying to find a specific house."

Deborah nodded. Brenna had always been a timid child. Because of this, people sometimes underestimated her, but as her mother, she'd always known Brenna was smart. In this situation, her daughter had reacted perfectly. She'd sensed that this man had an unhealthy interest in her and was in fact following her. In an act of self-preservation, she ran off and lost him.

Deborah had hope now, hope that her child was okay.

Roger spoke up. "How do you know he was telling the truth?"

Detective Zagon shrugged. "Honestly, his actions don't fit the profile of a kidnapper. He has no priors, and we interviewed him thoroughly and kept at it until he cried. If he knew anything, he would have talked. I really think he's just an idiot who saw Brenna and thought he could make some easy cash."

"So now what?" Cece asked.

"We keep looking," Detective Zagon said. "And we don't stop until we bring your sister home."

CHAPTER 21

*H*arry hadn't walked the streets of Manhattan to this degree since he was in his twenties. Walking, he'd always felt, was a waste of time. Exercise was done on the squash court or when using the equipment in his home gym. Leaving his building and going out on the sidewalk was something he only did to meet the car once his driver had pulled up to the curb. Going for miles on foot and stopping random people was far out of his usual routine, but if it meant bringing his daughter home, he'd do it all night.

After so many attempts, he finally realized the best lead-in was calling out to people as he approached, while holding up his cell phone. It helped, too, when he said, "Please, I need help. My daughter is missing. Have you seen her?" This worked well, especially with women. Women of all ages. It didn't matter if they looked like high school students or senior citizens. Most stopped and at least glanced at the photo. He hadn't encountered even one of them who'd seen Brenna, but at least they gave it a try. He was offered prayers and sympathy and good luck. One young woman asked, "If I do see her, what should I do?" Harry was impressed by how she'd thought ahead. Very clever.

"Don't let her walk away," he'd said. "Call the police and tell them you've found Brenna Vanderhaven." He'd thought for sure she'd know the name, but she'd repeated it slowly as if to press it into her memory. Maybe his family wasn't as famous as he'd thought.

Men, too, stopped to take a look, but the women were the ones who seemed most empathetic.

Walking for so many hours gave him time to think. If he'd wandered off like this at Brenna's age, upon his return home he would have gotten the beating of his life, accompanied by a verbal haranguing about his worth as a human being. His father liked to employ words like *worthless, brain-dead, idiot.* Another thing he liked to tell Harry was that he was a mistake. *It would have been better if you'd never been born.* Horrible words spoken by a horrible human being. Even with all the time that had elapsed, he could still clearly hear his father's words ringing in his ears.

The old man had softened over the years, which only meant he wasn't quite as overtly cruel as he'd been during Harry's youth, but he never was warm and caring. When he'd died in his early eighties, it had been a huge relief. A weight lifted. Looking at his father in the casket, one thought came to his mind: *You can't hurt me anymore.* But of course, that wasn't entirely true. The echoes of childhood had followed him into adulthood. Maybe, he mused, crossing the street in the midst of a sea of pedestrians, the pain of his childhood explained why he was so obsessed with building his fortune. Inside, he was still a little boy trying to prove he wasn't worthless.

He was so intent on scanning the streets for Brenna and asking those passing by if they'd seen her that he didn't spot the reporter until a microphone was thrust in his face. "Mr. Vander-haven," the fresh-faced young woman said. "Nedra Owens from

Channel 4 News." She was young, with dark skin and sleek hair that fell over her shoulders. A cameraman next to her had a large camera hoisted on one shoulder.

Although he was no stranger to reporters, he was taken aback. Usually he'd walk past these kinds of people, saying, "No comment," or he'd refer them to his attorney. Of course, that was when they wanted information about his business dealings.

She continued, "I understand that your daughter Brenna is missing?" She said it with a sympathetic camera-ready smile that revealed perfect teeth.

He hesitated only for an instant. "That's correct. I'm actually out here right now looking for her." He held up his phone, showing the reporter the photo. "She was last seen this afternoon leaving our apartment building on Central Park West and heading toward Columbus Circle."

By answering one question, he'd opened the door to an interview. From there, Nedra asked question after question, and he answered simply and truthfully. He gave a description of his daughter and confirmed that, yes, Brenna may have been upset when she left. She'd misunderstood something she'd overheard, he explained.

"And what was it that she overheard?" Nedra asked, her chin tipped up.

She acted concerned, but Harry wasn't falling for it. Instead of getting into more detail, he steered the conversation back to his daughter. "I'm sure you can understand that the important thing here is finding my daughter and bringing her home. The events leading up to her leaving are a family matter."

"The police were seen at your apartment earlier today. The usual police procedure is to wait forty-eight hours before investigating a report of a missing person. Are they making an exception for your family?"

This was where she was going?

"Actually, this isn't a case of preferential treatment. The

forty-eight-hour rule applies to adults." As a news reporter, she should have known that. Harry continued. "We notified the police because my eight-year-old daughter is missing and may be in danger. Obviously, the police have many pressing cases, and we understand that, which is why my older daughter, Cece, has asked her followers to be on the lookout as well. I'm sure you understand how worried we are, as worried as anyone would be if they weren't sure of the whereabouts of their child."

"Of course." Nedra nodded, but then she went off course again. "Speaking of Cece, there have been a lot of changes in your household. Recently, Cece parted ways with her good friends Vance and Katrina, and there are rumors she's going to be making big changes in her company as well. Is it possible that these changes are somehow connected with Brenna's disappearance?"

Harry had learned that the best way to answer intrusive questions was not to answer them at all. "Brenna walked out on her own and told the doorman she was taking a walk. He said she was alone and seemed fine. Our focus now is on finding her and bringing her home. I'm sure you can understand."

"Of course, but do you think—"

"Do you mind if I say something to my daughter?" he asked pleasantly but firmly, gesturing to the microphone. "Please?"

"Certainly." She thrust the microphone toward him. "Go ahead."

He looked imploringly toward the camera. "Brenna, if you see this, honey, your mom and Cece and I love you, and we miss you very much. All we want is for you to come home. And if anyone else has information that would help us find my daughter, please call the police immediately." He paused. "Oh, and thank you to everyone who has offered prayers and kind words. It means so much."

A yellow taxi pulled up to the curb eight feet away from where they stood. An elderly gentleman wearing a flat cap got out, then extended his hand for a silver-haired woman wearing a pleated striped dress. Nedra moved the microphone close to her mouth and said, "You and your wife are known to spend several weeks in Paris this time of year. Did you cut your trip short because of the viral video of your daughter Cece falling into the pond in Central Park?"

Harry held up one finger. "If you'll excuse me, I have somewhere I have to be." He jogged over to the taxi and slid through the open door before the older man had a chance to close it. His phone rang as he pulled the door shut. He spoke to the driver through the partition opening. "Could you please just drive somewhere while I take this call?"

"Somewhere?" The man turned to meet his gaze. "It doesn't matter?" His voice was tinged with the slightest of accents.

"Just go." He waved an impatient hand. "I'll let you know in a minute. I just need to take this call first."

The cab drove off as he turned his attention to his phone. It was Cece. He answered the way he always did. "Yes?"

As Cece told him that Brenna had been confirmed taking the subway to Park Slope, Brooklyn, that afternoon, he felt his chest relax like a balloon losing air. At least they knew where she'd been heading. "She never got to Nanny's house, and Nanny has no idea where she might have gone, but the police are widening their search area to include Park Slope. Greta and Dalton are at Nanny's place right now."

"What about the guy who wanted to trade information for five thousand dollars?"

"The detectives took him in for questioning but he didn't really know anything."

"I see." When Deborah had filled him in on this new development with CoolManLuke, he'd agreed that the guy didn't sound like a serious threat, but it was still a relief to know for sure. "Tell your mom I'm going to head over to Park Slope now and stop in at Margaret's house."

"You don't really need to," Cece said. "They'll let us know." Her voice became quieter. "I think Mom would like it if you came home."

"Let me talk to her."

"Hello. Harry?"

His dear wife—even under the worst circumstances, her voice was sweet and kind, something he'd always adored about her. Cece took after her mother that way as well. "Sweetheart, I wish I could be two places at once, but I wouldn't be able to sit at home knowing Brenna's still out there. I'd like to go to Margaret's and touch base with her, then look around the neighborhood. Does that sound like a good plan to you?"

"Of course. Whatever you want."

"I'll call and let you know as soon as I get there. Love you."

"I love you too."

"Can you have Cece text me Margaret's address?"

On the way to Brooklyn, Harry found his gaze permanently aimed at the world outside his window, looking, searching. He knew Brenna was unlikely to be in this in-between space, the bridge between Manhattan and Park Slope, but it gave him something to focus on. The bridge stretched on and on, longer than he remembered. He felt the old familiar impatience rising within him. When the driver made it into Brooklyn and finally stopped in front of a nondescript three-story brownstone, Harry said, "This is it?"

"Yes, sir. This is the address you gave me."

Harry swiped his credit card through the slot on the back of the seat, adding a generous 50 percent tip out of gratitude. "Thank you. I appreciate it."

He got out and trotted up the steps, then knocked loudly. The door swung open, revealing Margaret dressed more casually than he'd ever seen her. "Margaret," he said anxiously. "I hope you don't mind the intrusion at this late hour. You haven't heard from Brenna?" He knew the answer but had to ask.

"No." She shook her head. "I wish I could say otherwise, but I haven't."

"Oh." He stood there. "I was hoping you'd know something."

She tilted her head sympathetically. "I think we all would have liked that. Please, come on in."

Behind her stood Greta and Dalton. He felt oddly like he'd crashed a party as Margaret ushered all of them into the living room.

"You probably heard this already, but a woman on the subway talked to her, and she was coming to Park Slope to see you," he said, taking a seat. "And another man actually saw her in your neighborhood."

"We know—Cece called to tell us, and a police officer has already come by to ask a few questions. I really didn't have anything to tell him, I'm sorry to say." Her expression, her voice, everything about her said she felt the loss as much as he did.

Harry couldn't let it go. "Maybe she tried calling you? Maybe left a message?"

"I checked. She didn't call. I'm not sure she even knows my number."

Harry asked, "Could she have knocked on your door and you didn't hear it?"

Margaret shook her head. "I think she would have kept knocking until I answered. I would have heard it."

"Do you have any theories about where she might be? Maybe somewhere in Park Slope where you two would go together? A park or an ice cream parlor?" Were there still ice cream parlors? Harry wasn't sure. As a child, his own nanny used to take him out for ice cream sundaes at an ice cream parlor, but that was a long time ago, and he couldn't remember seeing one in ages. At any rate, a business like that wouldn't be open this late at night.

"I went over this with the police officer who was just here," Margaret said. "When she was little, I sometimes took her to the Third Street Playground in Prospect Park, but she's outgrown that. Usually we just hang out here. She likes helping me with my potted plants and baking cookies. And playing with my cats, of course. You know how much she loves animals."

Harry nodded and looked around the room. All three of the faces staring back reflected the frustration and worry he himself was feeling. "This is the worst day of my life," he said. "I've never felt so helpless. I'd do anything to get her back."

CHAPTER 22

The room fell into an awkward silence. Greta felt as if she should make some small talk or offer her sympathies, but Dalton was the one who spoke up first, mentioning that they'd met once before at his father's office.

"You're John Bishop's son?" Mr. Vanderhaven said, making the connection. "I've heard good things about you. Everyone says you're as aggressive and business savvy as your father. Good for you. Your father is a fierce competitor."

"I think you're referring to my older brother. I haven't been involved in the family business until recently, but I'm going to be heading up the Bishop Foundation. Our goal going forward is to help the homeless population in New York, primarily focusing on military veterans."

Mr. Vanderhaven nodded. "That sounds like a worthy pursuit. Someone's got to get the homeless off the streets. Their presence doesn't reflect well on our city, and from a financial standpoint it affects tourism."

"I was thinking more along the lines of helping a worthy group of people find their way back into society. They deserve health and happiness as much as anyone else does."

"Ah, I take your point."

Greta was surprised by how quickly Mr. Vanderhaven conceded to Dalton. She watched as the older man leaned over and rested his elbows on his knees. Cece had always spoken about her dad as if he had an imposing presence, but Greta was seeing a different side of him. She'd heard him say he felt helpless. That's how all of them felt.

"I'm sure she'll turn up soon," Greta said, hoping to ease his mind. "Cece has all of New York looking for her."

"I hope you're right," he said. "If someone hurts her . . ." His shoulders slumped in defeat.

Dalton spoke up then. "I can't even imagine what you're going through, but we don't have any reason to think she's been harmed. My dad always says it doesn't help to pre-worry."

Mr. Vanderhaven gave him a sad smile. "That's where we differ. I was brought up to worry ahead of time, just in case." He sighed.

The air in the room was heavy with emotion.

"I've been thinking . . . ," Greta said, then hesitated, wondering if she would be speaking out of turn.

"Yes?" Mr. Vanderhaven gave her his full attention. "You have an idea?"

"We know Brenna was heading this way, but she got off at the wrong stop. My guess is that she wasn't quite sure how to get here." She looked to Nanny, who nodded. "And if that's the case, she might still be walking around, lost. Or maybe she stopped somewhere to rest? I know the police are looking, but it can't hurt to have more eyes out there. We've been here for hours already. I feel like it's not doing much good for all of us to be sitting here and waiting."

Dalton took her hand. "Why don't the two of us head out and search?"

Greta stood up. "I agree. Let's do it."

Mr. Vanderhaven said, "I think that's an excellent idea,

Greta. I was planning on looking around the neighborhood myself."

Margaret went to pull Mr. Vanderhaven into a hug, and he let her. "You know I love Brenna too," she said. "If I can do anything, let me know. Whatever you need me to do."

He said, "We are lucky to have you as part of our family."

Greta watched this exchange, amazed at the words coming out of Mr. Vanderhaven's mouth. Cece had told her that her father had cautioned them about getting too close to the household staff, quoting him as saying, "They're not your friends. We pay them a fair wage to do a job, and that's the end of it. Don't get complacent and think they won't repeat things you say to the media. Most of them would sell you out for a hundred dollars." And now he was calling Margaret a member of the family.

All three said their goodbyes to Margaret, then headed out. Once on the sidewalk, Greta and Dalton agreed to cover the streets in the blocks between Nanny's place and the park, while Mr. Vanderhaven said he'd go in the opposite direction.

As they watched him walk away, Greta said, "Don't you feel a little bit sorry for him? We have each other, but he's all alone."

Dalton shrugged. "It makes more sense to split up. We can cover more ground that way."

"If that's the case, then why don't we split up?" She knew the answer. They didn't want to be apart. She just wanted to hear what he'd say.

"You're from Wisconsin. There are no cow pastures or breweries to mark the way for you. We don't need to have two people who are lost."

Greta laughed. "Nice try. Admit it—you just like to hang out with me." She gave his shoulder a playful poke.

"It's true. I'm not going to lie." He took her hand, and they continued on down the sidewalk. Greta found herself looking at every porch, underneath parked cars, and behind the short walls adjacent to the sidewalk. Off in the distance, they heard Harry Vanderhaven shouting Brenna's name.

"You think we should be yelling for her?" Greta asked.

Dalton said, "I don't know. Maybe. Part of me says we shouldn't disrupt the whole neighborhood. Kids might be sleeping. And part of me thinks that a missing child takes precedence."

They compromised, calling out Brenna's name once or twice on every block. Loud enough to be heard, but falling short of yelling. When they encountered other pedestrians, they showed them Brenna's picture, but no one had seen her. When they came across a young couple walking behind a little boy on the tiniest two-wheeled bike Greta had ever seen, Dalton showed the photo to the parents first, then stooped down to show the child. "Hi, Grayson. Have you seen this little girl today? Her name is Brenna."

The little boy, his hair covered by a zebra-print bike helmet, shook his head.

"Okay, thanks," Dalton said, rising to his feet. To the parents he said, "If you happen to spot her, call 911."

As they continued on, Greta said, "How did you know the kid's name?"

"You didn't hear his mom yelling, 'Grayson, you're getting too far ahead of us,' all the way down the block?" He grinned.

"Nope. I guess I wasn't paying attention." She pushed a lock of hair away from her face. "It was nice of you to show Grayson the picture."

"I wasn't just being nice. Kids are observant. He might have seen her."

The beginning stages of a romantic relationship were always the best, to Greta's mind. Both sides were so thoughtful of each other; odd quirks were charming rather than annoying. She knew this from her own life and also from countless hours listening to girlfriends talk about their love interests. The back-and-forth she experienced between herself and Dalton fit into this mold, but it felt different from what she'd known in the past. There was an ease in being with him. Neither one seemed to be trying too hard. She could own her inadequacies and not fear being mocked or looked down upon. Dalton, too, was relaxed with her—not trying to impress her and never upstaging others. Dalton was just Dalton, and she liked what she saw.

The fact that he worried they might be disturbing young families showed a foresight she hadn't seen in other guys his age. Of course, Grayson and his parents were out for a walk, which showed that not every kid went to bed that early. She'd found the way Dalton had knelt down and talked to Grayson touching. Clearly, he was good with children, which was promising. Greta was only twenty-three, so it was way too early to think about marriage and kids. It was on her list, though, and it didn't hurt to think ahead.

As they covered the miles, she took note of the way he kept pace with her own steps, considerably shorter than his own, and how he searched for Brenna as diligently as if she were his own cousin. His good qualities were many. Considerate, kind, good-looking. She could see this infatuation easily evolving into love. Right now she stood on the brink of it, but she wasn't going to take a step closer unless she felt he was there too. No point in rushing what could eventually blossom into something real in the future.

Not that long ago, the idea of spending the summer in New York had seemed like a huge adventurous leap. She'd wondered how she'd go so long without her family and friends. New York was foreign to her; Wisconsin was home. Already New York had opened her eyes and broadened her world, and home didn't seem as far away as she'd anticipated. Between Skype and texting and social media, she'd kept a toe dipped into the waters of her old life. The distance was not as extreme as she'd once thought.

Now her mind ventured to the idea of moving to New York permanently. Could she? Cece would give her a job and a place to live, she knew that much. Back home she'd be reduced to sending out résumés and going for interviews.

She felt a twinge of guilt, realizing she was mentally deliberating the pros and cons of moving to New York while her cousin was still missing. She needed to keep her thoughts focused on finding Brenna. Not doing so felt disloyal.

They rounded a corner, and Greta was delighted to see one shiny helium balloon bobbing above a wrought-iron railing. As they got closer, she could see it had been tied to the handrail and that it said "Happy First Birthday!" above the image of a cake. "Aww," she said in a way usually reserved for puppies and kittens. "Someone had their first birthday. How adorable is that?"

"I don't know about adorable. I've always thought that the first birthday is kind of a shocker," Dalton said, going up the steps and giving the balloon a tap.

"Why do you say that?"

"If you've never had a birthday before, all of it is unexpected. A cake with fire on it? Whoa! Gifts with bows? Fancy! The house festooned with crepe paper and balloons? Such a transformation! If you didn't know better, you'd think your whole family had gone crazy and decided you were the center of the universe."

"Well, when you put it that way, it does sound a little bit out there."

"And then there's the second birthday. Same old, same old. It's like, *Oh, now we're doing this again.*" He came down and joined her on the sidewalk, crooking his elbow and waiting for her grasp. "Let's keep going."

When they got to the end of the block, she said, "Last year I read the best book. It was about a little nine-year-old boy who ran away from home. He didn't mean to run away; it just happened."

"So he *accidentally* ran away?"

"Sort of. He was running away from a beating by his alcoholic father and hid in a moving truck parked on his street. The back was open, and he just sort of slid inside and then was trapped when the doors went down and the driver took off. He wound up hours away from home."

"Sounds exciting."

"Not exciting, exactly." She paused to think. "A lot of people helped him along the way, and it had a happy ending. It was heartwarming."

"Huh. *Heartwarming* is not the word I would have matched with a kid getting beaten by his alcoholic father."

"That was just the jumping-off point to the plot. I wouldn't have read it if it had been a violent, dark story. The world has enough bad news. I like positive fiction, books where kindness prevails. I guess I'm kind of hoping that Brenna comes upon some kind people who help her find her way home."

"Greta Hansen, you are an exceptionally good person."

"No," she said, shaking her head. "Just average."

"Not true. I know a lot of people, and believe me, if average is the planet Earth, you're the equivalent of another galaxy. You have to know you're really special."

She gave him a shy sideways glance, blushing because she was definitely not used to such praise. None of the guys she knew were capable of giving much more than a standard compliment. This was far beyond that. She said, "I'm certainly glad that you think so."

CHAPTER 23

When Brenna woke up, the room was dark; the only visible light came in from the open door leading to the hallway. She sat up, momentarily bewildered. It was only after she spotted Summer standing in the corner of the room that she remembered all that had transpired since she left home.

"What time is it?" she asked, glancing around the room. There was no clock in sight.

"Shh." Summer held a finger to her lips. "We have to be quiet. My mom and dad are asleep." She came over to the foot of the bed and rested her hand on Baxter, who slept there curled up like a comma. He whined slightly, his eyes still closed.

Summer's mom and dad were asleep? Brenna rubbed her eyes and thought of her own parents. Certainly by now they'd noticed she was gone. Were they worried? They'd never worried about her before, not that she knew of, anyway, but she'd never gone off by herself either. "I have to go home," she said, her eyes tearing up. "I want my mom and dad." Thinking for a minute, she added, "I'm hungry, and I miss my sister."

"Don't cry," Summer said. "Please don't cry. I know something that will help." She crooked one finger and backed up to the door. "Come on."

Brenna sniffed, then followed her out of the room and down the hallway. The light she'd seen before was actually a series of night-lights in every outlet along the way. Summer led her down the stairs, her hand on the railing to guide her, and Brenna trailed behind. At the bottom, Brenna could see a light coming from the living room and the room ahead. Before she could ask if someone was awake, Summer said, "My mom likes to leave lights on at night."

Their trek ended in the kitchen. The room wasn't nearly as big as either of the kitchens at Brenna's house, but it was tidy and bright. The under-cabinet lights were on, casting a glow onto the shiny quartz countertops and illuminating the light-brown cabinets and their painted knobs. A bowl of fruit next to the stove held bananas and one lonely avocado. The refrigerator had double doors with shiny handles and a big drawer at the bottom. A small island sat in the middle of the room, fronted by three barstools. A few feet behind the stools sat a kitchen table surrounded by six ladder-backed chairs.

Brenna said, "I thought you were going to get someone to help me." She glanced at the counters, looking for a phone, but there was only an iPad plugged into a charger.

"You said you were hungry. Don't you want to have something to eat first?"

Brenna's stomach rumbled. Food would help. She looked up at the balloons hung from the pendant lights over the island, and the twisted crepe paper that swooped in from the edges of the room, meeting in the middle like a carousel. "Cool decorations," she said.

"My mom always does this for birthdays."

Brenna's mom always had other people do the birthday decorations, and she had Nanny order a cake, any flavor Brenna wanted. She could choose how the cake was decorated as well.

Brenna always had a kid party of her choosing and went out to dinner with her parents and Cece. They never celebrated in their apartment. Her dad said kids were too boisterous and liable to make a mess.

Summer said, "If you want something to eat, there are sandwiches in the fridge." She pointed. "Drinks too."

"After that I need to go home." Brenna wanted to go home more than anything, but her stomach growled again, reminding her she was starving, hungrier than she ever remembered being in her entire life. "But I guess I could eat something first." She waited for Summer to open the refrigerator, but when the little girl made no move to do so, she said, "Can I just help myself?"

After Summer nodded, Brenna opened the door to find a tray of sub sandwiches, wrapped in clear wrap. She peeled back a corner and grabbed a sandwich, then replaced the plastic wrap. In the door she noticed cans of soft drinks. After checking out all her options, she nabbed a root beer, then joined Summer at the island counter. "I feel like I shouldn't be here," she said, popping open the can and looking around the room. She lowered her voice to a whisper. "Your mom and dad are going to catch us, and they're gonna be mad that I'm here."

Summer's little shoulders came up in a shrug. "They won't wake up. Not if we're quiet."

"But they'd be mad if they knew I was in your house, right?"

"I don't think so."

Brenna took a bite of her sandwich, tearing at the bread with her teeth. The one she'd chosen turned out to be turkey with lettuce, tomato, and some kind of white cheese. Paired with a slug of root beer, it was just what she needed. Her stomach began to settle as she ate more of the sandwich, and she started to feel less anxious about Summer's parents. Even if she was a trespasser, she was only a child and had been invited inside by their own daughter. Once they were awake, they would surely help her find her way home. When she was done, she brushed the crumbs off the front of her shirt and got up off her barstool to carry the empty root beer can to the sink. "Can you wake up your parents now?" she asked Summer. "And ask them to help me?"

Summer pursed her lips. "I don't think I can wake them up."

"Why not?"

"I just can't."

"What if I do it?"

"If you want. They're probably not going to like it. My dad has a baseball bat next to their bed. He keeps it there in case bad guys break into the house. If you wake him up, he might just grab it and come after you."

Brenna considered this scenario. She was pretty sure she could outrun a man who had just been woken out of a sound sleep. Besides, he'd quickly see how little she was and that she was just a kid. She definitely wasn't a criminal. "I guess I have to take that chance."

Back up the stairs they went, with Baxter on their heels. Summer led the way to her parents' room on the far end of the hallway opposite of her own. As they walked past a closed door, she pointed out that it was her brother's room. "Oliver sleeps through the night most of the time now, but sometimes when he can't sleep, I go in to sing to him. He likes it when I pretend his toy turtle can talk."

The door to Summer's parents' room was halfway open. Brenna followed Summer in, hanging back a bit. The light from the hallway night-lights cast a dim glow, and when her eyes adjusted, she could see Summer's mom sleeping on the side closest to the door, with her husband next to her facing the other direction. Just as Summer had said, a baseball bat was propped against the wall on his side, only an arm's reach from where he slept.

Brenna, who'd been feeling brave in the kitchen, had a change of heart. Maybe it was the dark, or the fact that she didn't know these people, but she suddenly lost her nerve. Sensing this, Summer took the lead, putting her hand on her mom's shoulder. "Mommy? Can you wake up?" She put a hand across her mother's forehead, and the woman sighed in her sleep.

"Summer?" she mumbled.

"Yes, it's me. This is my friend, Brenna. She needs help to get home."

"Oh, sweetie." The words came out in one soft breath.

"Mommy? Do you hear me? My friend needs help."

Brenna leaned in closer, watching carefully. Summer's mom shifted in her sleep, and her lips moved, but no sound came out. Sometimes during thunderstorms when she was younger Brenna used to climb into bed with her sister, and Cece would do the same kind of thing. Cece often muttered and shifted around while sound asleep; once while her eyes were still closed, Cece had even held the covers up for Brenna to climb under. She'd been sleeping so soundly that in the morning she'd had no recollection of doing so and was surprised to find her sister there. Brenna reached down to touch the woman's shoulder, but just before her fingertips made contact, Summer's mother rolled over in her sleep. Brenna pulled her hand back as if bitten. It just felt wrong. It wasn't her mother. She didn't know this woman.

Now all at once, a fearful unease came over her. She wasn't supposed to be here, in someone else's house. She never should have left her own home without permission. If she could go back in time, she would have mustered up the courage to knock on Cece's door, or better yet, stayed in her room as instructed.

She backed out of the room, gesturing for Summer to follow her. When they got to Summer's room, she whispered, "I think I'm just going to go." Her breathing was ragged, keeping pace with her frantic heartbeat. "I'm going to leave now and go look for a subway. I think I can find my way back. My mom and dad have to be missing me by now."

Summer's gaze dropped to the floor, and when she looked up, she quietly said, "They always miss you when you're gone."

"Thanks for the sandwich. You should go to bed. I know how to get to the front door." She went to the window and peered up and down the street. There was no sign of the creepy man being out there anymore.

Please don't go," Summer pleaded. "Stay right here and I'll go get my mom. I'll make sure she wakes up. Then she can call your mom."

Brenna hesitated. Even not knowing the time, she was pretty sure it was the middle of the night, and she knew it was very dark. Finding her way in the daylight had been difficult; doing it at this time would be that much harder. If Summer could get her mom to help, that would be much easier. "If you think you can wake her up."

Summer nodded, relief washing over her face. "I will."

"And then she'll help me get home?"

Summer smiled. "She likes to help people. She's the best mom in the world."

Brenna sat with her legs dangling over the side of the bed, watching as Summer disappeared through the open doorway. She lay down next to Baxter and reached over to stroke the dog's head. She scratched behind his ears, and Baxter yawned, then laid his head on his front paws. Her eyelids drooped, but she fought the urge to sleep. Summer would be back any minute with her mom.

She thought about how Summer's mother had looked with her eyes closed, murmuring her daughter's name. She seemed like a nice lady. Brenna was certain she'd help get her back home. Soon all would be well again.

CHAPTER 24

*C*allie awoke on the cusp of a wonderful dream. She kept her eyes closed to prolong the warm feeling. In the dream, her little daughter Summer had come to her while she slept, rested her hand on her forehead, and said she loved her. It had been so real; she had felt her little girl's breath on her face as she leaned over to kiss her cheek. She could hear her sweet voice calling her *Mommy*. Such a gift.

Oh, if only it were true.

With her eyes still shut, she rolled over and draped her arm over Colton. In the morning she'd tell him all about it. How often had they talked about it? Countless times. She'd accepted that Summer was gone. The pain of losing her was still there, not quite as raw or as constant but always under the surface. She'd once asked the leader of her grief group, an older woman named Joyce who'd lost a child herself, when the pain would go away, and she'd sadly shook her head and said never. "It never goes away. It morphs into something manageable. Eventually you can remember the good things and even smile and laugh at the memories, but you never really get over the loss. At least I never did."

Joyce had been right. There was no coming to terms with it, no getting over it. Somehow she continued on, doing what she had to do to live this life. She moved forward because she had to. Eventually she was even able to find some joy in life. But it was never the same.

The loss of a child was proof you could live with a broken heart.

When she became pregnant with Oliver, people assumed it would help, as if one child could replace the other. Oliver was a treasure, a gift after a long stretch of sadness. He was a healthy, happy baby and a delight to have around. Still, she couldn't help but think about how thrilled Summer would have been to have a baby brother. Summer had been a little mother to all of her dolls and stuffed animals. She comforted other children when they cried. Colton's mother had said Summer was an old soul. She had an empathy that was rare in children that age. She would have been a stellar older sister. Callie didn't have to do the math to know that now she'd be seven, in first grade. She tried to picture her at that age, but it was impossible. Summer would always be four, almost five, incapable of anything but goodness. Callie knew all mothers had high opinions of their children, but others had agreed that her daughter was special. At the funeral, one of Summer's teachers said she'd never seen a child so thoughtful and caring. "One day she asked me if my head hurt, and I actually did have a headache at the time. I couldn't believe she picked up on that. Believe me, I've worked with kids for more than twenty years, and she was one of a kind."

Little did people know how much hearing these kinds of stories eased her grief. She'd kept all the cards and notes that arrived after Summer's death. She appreciated each and every one, especially the personal notes that mentioned something specific about her daughter. The woman who cut Summer's hair sent flowers and a note saying, "Summer was well named because she brought sunshine wherever she went. I will miss her and her contagious laughter."

Knowing her daughter had made a difference during her short life was a balm to her soul.

Over the days, months, and years, Callie had accepted the loss, realized no one was to blame, and found ways to cope with Summer's death. The only thing she had wished for was a sign, something that indicated her daughter was in a good place. She watched for feathers and rainbows and all the other things people designated as signs, but nothing ever came. Colton said that Oliver was their sign. When she was pregnant, he'd stroked her belly and mused, "I can't imagine Summer would be the type of child who would be jealous of the baby. She would have loved him."

And now at long last she'd dreamed of Summer, felt her touch and heard her voice. If she hadn't known better, she'd have sworn Summer had actually been with her. A sign. She'd finally gotten her sign. Three years later and on the eve of her little brother's first birthday. Did that have some significance? Maybe.

She considered waking Colton up to tell him about the dream but decided against it. With a baby in the house, sleep was a rare commodity. She'd let her husband sleep and tell him over breakfast.

Baxter came into their room and let out a low whine. He wasn't allowed on their bed. That had been Colton's rule, but after Summer died, they hadn't stopped the dog from sleeping on Summer's bed. Even now, years later, he liked to hang out in her old room, still exactly as it had been when she'd passed away. The only exception had been the closet and dresser drawers. Callie had cleaned out all the clothing when her mother had suggested it would be a nice tribute to Summer to donate her things to a program for families in need. Knowing that Summer had liked to share made it easier.

Baxter gave a low, quiet bark, and Callie rolled over and draped her arm over the side of the bed to rub behind his ears. She glanced at the clock on her nightstand. Four forty in the morning. Good grief, it was early. She pulled her hand back, hoping that quick pet would satisfy Baxter, but when he whined again, running to the doorway and coming back to face her, she knew he wanted to be let outside. "Give me a second," she muttered, rubbing her eyes. Almost on autopilot, she rose from the bed, put on her slippers, and grabbed her robe off the hook in the closet. Having a full night's sleep was a rarity. If it wasn't the baby, it was the dog.

"You got this, babe?" Colton asked, half-asleep.

She slipped her arms into the sleeves and secured the tie around her middle. "Yeah, I'll take care of him. Go back to sleep, honey." Soon enough Oliver would be awake, and there'd be no rest for either of them.

Baxter trotted out the door, and she followed slowly. When they got to the stairs, he bypassed it, going straight for Summer's room and pausing in the doorway. She stopped and whispered, "What are you doing? Let's go down." She pointed, and when he didn't move, she went down a few steps, thinking he would follow. When he didn't, she went back up the stairs to where he sat, his hindquarters tucked under him, his nose aimed into the room. "Come on, boy." She took his collar and gently tugged to get him to go with her, but instead he pulled her forward until both of them were next to Summer's bed.

The room was dark, the only light coming from the hallway behind her, but she could tell that the covers had been disturbed and were now mounded. In a second, her vision adjusted and she realized the mound was actually someone curled up on Summer's bed. A child. Her breath caught in her chest, and for a split second she thought that she hadn't woken up at all and that this was a continuation of her dream. But no, this felt too real.

Callie reached over to turn on the nightstand lamp and saw

that the child curled up on the bed wasn't Summer. The sudden shock of the light startled the girl, who sat up abruptly, a guilty look on her face. The two of them froze, both of them taking in the sight of the other. Baxter eased the moment by jumping up on the bed next to the little girl, who rested her hand on her back. "Are you Summer's mommy?" she finally asked.

"Yes." She was so taken aback that she could get out only the one word. No one had referred to her as Summer's mommy in a long time. How did this child even know Summer's name? Her mind raced, sifting through everything she knew and trying to make sense of this strange child in her daughter's bed. The girl was the right age to have been Summer's contemporary had she lived, but Callie didn't know this child. Besides, that wouldn't explain how she happened to be in their house in the middle of the night. Callie rubbed her eyes, thinking she might be hallucinating, but all of her senses told her this was real. "Who are you?"

"I'm Brenna," she said. "I got lost." Her lower lip quivered, and tears pooled in her eyes.

"Are you Brenna Vanderhaven?" Callie's mind reeled, so many thoughts running through her head.

The little girl nodded. "I want to go home. I miss my mom and dad."

Callie sat next to her on the bed and wrapped her arms around her. They'd get this sorted out very soon, but for now she was just a mother comforting a little girl. "It's okay, honey. I'll help you get home to your parents."

CHAPTER 25

*C*allie listened, dumbfounded, as Brenna related how she came to be in their house. The little girl talked so earnestly about the series of events that had brought her there, starting with her stop on the sidewalk in front of their house and ending with her falling asleep in Summer's bed. Although Callie could tell that to Brenna it all made sense, following along with her impossible story had her bewildered.

She had to hear this again. "So Summer tapped on the glass, and you looked up and saw her in the window?"

Brenna scrunched up her face, thinking. "I think Baxter jumped on the window, and that's when I looked up and Summer waved at me to come in. I wasn't going to, but I saw the creepy man on the sidewalk, and I was afraid."

"And then you came inside . . ."

"Yes, but Summer said I had to wait until the party was over to talk to you. I wanted to go home right away, but she said we should wait for Oliver to open his gifts."

"Oliver?"

"Her little brother? You know, the one having the party?"

"Of course." Callie managed a smile, even as her mind tried

to make sense of what she was being told. She had trouble reconciling what she knew to be true with what Brenna presented to her so matter-of-factly. She wanted to believe her, but her brain told her it was contrary to reason.

"I tried to wait, but I fell asleep." Brenna patted the comforter.

"Did Summer look like me? Solid?" Callie asked, making a show of tapping her own arm.

Brenna squirmed. "She looked a little like you, I guess. You're her mom, right, so you'd look kind of the same?"

"No, I mean did she look like a regular person, or could you see right through her like smoke or like a holographic image?"

"That's silly," Brenna said, amused. "You can't see through people."

"So she looked like a regular person? Like you or me?"

"Well, not so big as me because she's only four. Almost five." Brenna looked toward the door. "Is she still in your room?"

"Was she supposed to be in my room?"

"Well, yeah. She said she'd wake you up, for sure this time. We tried before, but you were fast asleep."

Callie got up and got the photo off the dresser. She still remembered the day it was taken. She and Colton and Summer had spent an idyllic day at the beach, playing in the sand and frolicking at the edge of the water. She hadn't known then there wouldn't be any more summer days at the beach with Summer. Holding out the picture, she asked, "So Summer looked just like this?"

Brenna bobbed her head up and down. "Except she wasn't wearing a swimming suit, of course."

Callie returned the picture to the dresser and went back to sitting next to Brenna. She tried to keep the conversation going, but Brenna didn't have much to add to what she'd already said. When it was clear Brenna was all talked out, Callie said, "I'm going to get my husband, okay? I'll just be gone a minute. He's a very nice man, and I'm sure he'll want to hear all about how Summer helped you."

"And then you'll call my mom and dad?"

"Yes, honey. Right after that." She held up one finger. "Don't move. I'll be right back."

She turned on the light and woke Colton, telling him he had to get up, it was important. They'd been married long enough that he didn't question it, just grabbed his bathrobe and followed her out into the hall. He started to head for Oliver's room, but she grabbed his arm and whispered, "This way."

Part of her thought that Brenna might not be there when they returned to the bedroom, but the little girl was right where she'd left her, legs hanging over the side of the bed, her hair tousled.

"This is my husband, Colton," she said. "Colton, this is Brenna Vanderhaven. She came inside with the birthday party guests yesterday afternoon and has been here ever since. She said Summer was at that window"—she pointed—"and motioned for her to come inside."

Colton's jaw dropped, and his gaze went from Brenna to his wife and back again. He was barely awake as it was, and she'd presented him with a story he couldn't wrap his brain around. She knew he was trying to process what she was telling him because she herself didn't half believe it. But why would Brenna lie? And how else would she know so much about her daughter and their house?

Colton finally spoke. "You're Brenna? Brenna Vanderhaven?"

"Yeah."

"And how did you get here?"

"I was lost, and then Summer waved to me and pointed to the door," Brenna explained. "I didn't really hear what she was saying 'cause the window was closed, but then when I was inside she said we shouldn't bother you because you were busy with Oliver's party. And then I fell asleep on the bed. And now I just want to go home."

Colton cleared his throat and gripped Callie's arm. He whispered, "How is this happening?"

She shook her head. "I don't know. I had a dream about Summer. It was so real. When I woke up, Baxter led me in here, and I found Brenna asleep on the bed."

Brenna said, "I was looking for my nanny's house when I got lost. I was walking and walking, and I was so tired and I was getting kind of scared, and then Summer let me use your bathroom, and I'm sorry but I ate one of your sandwiches when you were asleep. I drank a can of root beer too. She said it would be okay with you. She said her mom and dad were really nice."

Colton knelt on one knee in front of her. "What else did she say? I want to know everything she told you."

Brenna looked nervous. "She said that she had the best mom in the world." She gulped. "Summer said it was okay to be here. She said you wouldn't mind."

"You're not in any trouble," Callie said. "The things you're telling us are making us very happy."

A wash of relief came over Brenna's face. They asked her to start at the beginning, and she related everything in sequence, answering their questions about what Summer looked like and repeating everything she'd said. "She said her aunt Lauren thinks you're mad at her." Brenna gave Callie a wide-eyed look. "And she said her aunt is afraid that seeing her makes you sad. That's why she doesn't come around so much."

"Lauren thinks she makes me sad?" Callie asked.

Brenna nodded. "Summer said you said some things that made her feel bad."

The two exchanged a look. Callie said to her husband, "I apologized for that a long time ago. I thought we were okay. I mean, it's bad enough that we lost Summer. I don't want to lose my sister too."

"Lost Summer?" Brenna's face scrunched up, puzzled. "When did you lose Summer?"

Callie bit her lip, debating what to tell her, but Colton spoke first. "We didn't really lose her," he said. "She's with us every day."

When Colton went into the other room to get his cell phone, Callie took the hairbrush off the dresser. Except to lift it up when dusting, she hadn't touched it or used it since Summer passed away. The entire room had been left just as it had been the very day she'd died, quickly and unexpectedly, in her very own bed. Colton had suggested redecorating to make the room into a home office or a guest room, but Callie had resisted. Removing her daughter's space felt like erasing her existence, equivalent to saying she hadn't been a real person, that there'd never been a delightful sparkler of a child, one who had lived and laughed and twirled around right on the rug in front of the bed. She'd been the center of their universe. How could she just pack up Summer's things and get rid of them? It didn't feel right. Now she held on to the smooth wooden handle of the brush and asked Brenna, "While my husband is calling for help to get you home, how about I brush your hair so it looks pretty when you see your mom and dad?"

Brenna smiled shyly. "I would like that."

Callie was gently running the brush through her hair when Colton walked back into the room, the cell phone outstretched, screen up. He had it on speakerphone and was talking to a woman Callie assumed was the 911 operator.

"Yes," he said. "Brenna Vanderhaven is with my wife and me in our home in Park Slope. Apparently she's been here the whole night, but we didn't find her until just now." He answered all the operator's questions but never mentioned Summer's part in Brenna entering their house. It was just as well, Callie thought. She was finding it hard to believe. Anyone else would think them crazy for even considering it might be true.

Was it true? She wanted to think so. Otherwise, how was it that Brenna knew so much? She'd described what Summer looked like and gave details about the family that weren't publicly known. Where would she get that knowledge? How could a little eight-year-old girl from a prestigious family who lived in the Central Park West neighborhood know about the schism between herself and Lauren? There was no way. They didn't have anyone or anything in common.

She remembered coming home on that sad and awful day and finding Summer unresponsive. After that, the memory became a montage of horror: the frantic moments of calling 911, guiding the first responders into her room and watching them do CPR on her little girl. When they announced her baby girl was gone, her world had gone to a standstill. Everything after that—calling Colton at work, notifying the relatives, and the funeral—was a blur. It was as if her brain had shut off and her body went through the motions. A coping mechanism for an unspeakable tragedy. Everyone was sorry. Sympathies were offered and hugs and prayers, but none of it brought Summer back. Somewhere in there she'd said some horrible words to Lauren, but she had no distinct memory of it. When Lauren brought it up, she said she was sorry, even as she wasn't entirely sure what she was apologizing for.

Part of her resented Lauren for making it about her. She and Colton had lost a child, and Lauren wanted her to apologize for a few harsh words? Things she couldn't even remember saying? Clearly, she'd been out of her mind at the time. She'd blamed herself for Summer's death. Maybe if she'd been there things would have gone differently.

It happened on a Saturday afternoon. Callie had wanted to go shopping for Christmas presents. Since Colton had to go in to work, her sister had offered to watch Summer that day. This was an offer that was easy to say yes to. Lauren adored Summer, and the feeling was mutual. From what Callie was told later,

Lauren had taken Summer out to lunch, and when they came back to the house, Summer said she was tired, so Lauren had read to her in bed. When Summer drifted off, Lauren kissed her and tiptoed out of the room. "She looked like a little angel lying there," Lauren had said, bewildered. "She wasn't in pain or anything. Just tired. I thought she just needed a nap."

Summer had drifted off, and sometime in the next two hours, she'd died of an undiagnosed heart abnormality she'd had since birth. They didn't know that at the time, of course. She was just inexplicably, heartbreakingly gone.

Lauren was the last one to see Summer alive. The last one to kiss her sweet cheek. The last one to say, "I love you." While Summer slipped away, Callie had been shopping, of all things. She remembered hearing Christmas music playing as she picked out some expensive gloves for Colton. She'd anticipated how much he'd love them, the soft Italian leather and the smooth lining. In retrospect, it was all so silly. None of it mattered. She should have been home with her daughter that day. The fact that she hadn't been had made her angry. She was mad at herself and at God and the world in general. But the one who'd gotten the full force of her emotion was Lauren, just by virtue of having been there.

Callie's thoughts were interrupted by her husband handing her the phone. "She wants to talk to you," he said.

"Yes?" Callie turned off the speaker and put the phone up to her ear.

The 911 operator said, "You were the one who discovered Brenna Vanderhaven in your home?"

"That's right."

"We're sending two police officers to your residence. In the meantime, can you tell me how you came to find Brenna?"

"Of course." Callie told the story, starting with Baxter wanting to go out and ending with finding Brenna sleeping in the empty bedroom.

"And then what happened?"

"I was surprised to see her there, as you can imagine." Callie sucked in a sharp breath and then walked out of the room to answer. "I woke her up. Brenna told me her name and said she had been lost and tired. We had a birthday celebration for our one-year-old son yesterday evening. Brenna followed the guests into the house and went upstairs and fell asleep. We didn't discover her until just now." She knew that Colton had given her the same information, but she didn't mind repeating it. The woman was just doing her job.

"Does Brenna appear to be in good shape?"

"I guess so. She just misses her mom and dad and wants to go home." Callie glanced back into the room, where Colton was talking quietly to Brenna. Something about Summer. She wished she could hear.

The operator wanted to know what Brenna was wearing and if she and her husband knew the Vanderhavens or had any business dealings with them.

"Business dealings? No." Was she insinuating that they had kidnapped Brenna? Callie felt a little irate. "We just found her in our home. Honestly, that's what happened."

The doorbell rang, followed by a sharp rapping at the front door. Colton stood and went down the stairs to answer. She heard him taking two steps at a time. "I think the police are here at the front door." Callie stuck her head over the railing and saw two officers entering the house. "Yes, they're here."

"Okay, then we can end the call."

"Thank you for your help." She clicked off and went back to Brenna. "Come on, honey. I think the police are here to take you home."

CHAPTER 26

$\mathcal{H}$arry walked the dark streets of Park Slope for hours, giving him a lot of time to think. When he'd first arrived at Margaret's, Harry had been overwrought. It was only a slight relief to find out that everyone else there felt the same. All of them had found themselves at jittery loose ends, wanting to do something but not knowing exactly what to do. It was a relief when Greta suggested that the three of them leave to search the area. He knew it was probably because he seemed to be a nervous wreck. He sensed a kindness about her. "I'm sure she'll turn up soon," Greta had said, trying to reassure him. "Cece has all of New York looking for her."

Harry had nodded. "I hope you're right."

She meant well, he knew that, but what she didn't know was that as a seven-year-old child he had once been snatched by a would-be kidnapper. The man had grabbed him as he left the building where he took music lessons. There was a twenty-foot distance between the door and his waiting nanny, and in that space, he'd been grabbed by his collar, yanked off his feet, and dragged to a waiting car. They'd pulled away before his nanny, a nice young woman named Miss Rawson, could react. He'd found out later that the two men—one in the driver's seat, the other holding on to him in the back seat—were brothers and that they'd planned to ransom him for a million dollars, but they were never able to carry out their plan because he was able to wriggle free from the man's grasp.

Pushing the door open, he'd jumped out of the car as it turned a corner, losing his balance in the process and falling to the street. His elbow and knees were torn up, the skin raw and bleeding. He was lucky he hadn't hit his head. The incident had been traumatic, but his own father had found the story hilarious and blamed him for letting it happen. "A big boy like you and you couldn't stop him from putting you in a car?" he'd said. "Why didn't you fight?"

His father's comments had made him feel ashamed, as if the whole thing had been his fault.

After that he was always on high alert, and as an adult, he'd orchestrated the lives of his wife and daughters with safety in mind. Greta had no way of knowing this. She was from a nice middle-class family in the Midwest. Deborah had been the same way when he'd first met her. Someone of that background would not even be able to fathom the dangers that were out there for families of wealth. There was a cost to their privilege. There was always someone who wanted what they had. Too, there were those who held grudges against his rather ruthless but necessary business practices.

Walking was a good antidote to the anxiety spreading in his chest. He took measured steps and called out Brenna's name at least once per block. He found himself peering around shrubbery and checking every stoop. When he rounded the corner at the end of the block, he saw two figures, a man and a woman, heading toward him. With a start, he recognized Greta and Dalton.

"Any luck?" he called out. He knew the answer but still had to ask.

"No," Dalton said, while Greta just shook her head sadly. "You?"

"Not yet."

They stood across from each other, keeping their voices low. Greta said, "We're wondering if we should head back and check the playground equipment? There would be hiding places there, and it would be familiar, so it might feel like a safe spot."

"Maybe," Harry said. He wasn't ready to discount anything. "But if she found the park, wouldn't she know the way to and from Margaret's house from the park?"

"Possibly," Greta admitted.

"I'm not saying it's a bad idea. I'm just thinking it through."

Dalton said, "We can head back that way and search if you want us to."

Before he could answer, Harry's phone rang. When he saw it was Deborah, his mood tentatively lifted. *Please let it be that they found Brenna. Please.* Before putting the phone up to his ear, he told them, "It's my wife."

Greta held on to Dalton's arm. "I hope it's good news."

"Yes?" Harry said.

Deborah said, "They found her!"

"Oh, thank you, God." He put his hand to his chest. "Where is she? What happened?" Greta and Dalton, hearing the good news secondhand, collectively sighed in relief. Dalton wrapped his arms around Greta, and she leaned into him.

His wife told him Brenna was safe and hadn't been harmed. "I talked to her. She sounded a little shaken up, but she's not hurt. After she got off the subway, she just wandered around looking for Nanny's house and got hopelessly lost. She wound up following some guests into a house having a birthday party."

"And they didn't notice a strange child at the party?" Harry asked.

"Brenna didn't join the party," Deborah explained. "She

followed their daughter upstairs and fell asleep on one of the beds. The lady of the house found her there this morning."

"That's so bizarre." Harry thought it sounded like the stuff of fairy tales. He imagined the media would have a field day if they heard about this, with a headline something like *Brenna Vanderhaven Pulls a Goldilocks*. Back in the day—the day being only the day before—the idea that his family might get this kind of news coverage would have bothered him. Now, he shrugged it off. Let people talk. What did it matter?

"Bizarre, but at least she's safe. It could have been much worse."

He exhaled. Deborah went on, telling him the address of the home. It was a townhouse in Park Slope. He repeated the location, and Dalton said, "That's not too far from here."

"Apparently that's close to where I am now. I'm going to head over there as soon as we hang up," Harry told Deborah. "Tell the police to wait, that I'm coming to take her home. I don't want them to frighten her."

After ending the conversation, he turned to the others, tears in his eyes. This show of feelings wasn't like him. He hadn't felt so overpowered by emotion in many years. He tried unsuccessfully to shake it off, to give the appearance of a man in charge, but he couldn't manage it.

"She's fine, not hurt. Nothing bad happened. She just got lost." He swallowed, gratitude blooming in his chest. "She followed some birthday party guests into someone's house and fell asleep on their daughter's bed. The parents didn't discover her until just now."

"Good news," Greta said with a smile.

"I can't thank you enough," Harry said. "For all your caring and your time and the way you walked the streets searching for my daughter . . ." His voice broke. "You've been up all night, and you've walked for hours. You went way beyond what most people would do."

"We were glad to help," Dalton said. "And we're relieved this has a happy ending."

"I was worried sick, and I know it was even worse for you," Greta said. "I'm so happy it's over with and she's okay."

Harry said, "Would you mind taking me to the address?"

"Of course, Mr. Vanderhaven," Dalton said. "We'd be happy to."

He gave an appreciative look. "Thank you. Oh, and please, from now on, call me Harry."

"All right, Harry. This way."

He stuck the phone in his back pocket and followed behind Dalton and Greta, who led him to the end of the block. Once they rounded the corner, they saw a police car pull in front of a house thirty feet ahead. A quick glance confirmed they were in front of the address he'd been heading toward. As they got out of the car, he approached them. "Hi, I'm Harry Vanderhaven. I'm assuming you're here for my daughter, Brenna?"

CHAPTER 27

W hen Detective Thompson had called Deborah earlier, he'd started the conversation by saying he had good news. Brenna had been found by a family in Park Slope. Hearing that her daughter was safe was the sweetest news in the world. She would never take her family for granted again. As she spoke to the detective, Cece had gestured to her to put the call on speakerphone, but Deborah held up a hand to stop her. She was too overcome with emotion to do two things at once. She could only listen.

She hadn't realized how tightly she'd tensed her muscles until she'd finished the phone call. Then her entire body had turned to jelly. She knew now why those giving surprising news prefaced it by asking if the other party was sitting down.

After she hung up with the detective, she gave Cece and Roger an explanation of what had happened. "Brenna is fine. The guy who was following her never touched her. She's been in one spot the whole time, a house in Park Slope. She followed some birthday party guests inside and then fell asleep on a bed upstairs. It sounds like the couple didn't realize their daughter had invited her inside. I would guess that with all the excitement of the party, they were distracted."

"Oh, thank you, God," Cece said. Her words echoed exactly what Deborah was feeling.

Roger whistled and shook his head in an appreciative way. "Now that's a happy ending. I'm so glad."

Her next course of action was to call Harry with the good news. After they'd hung up she told Cece, "Your dad is going to bring Brenna home." A simple statement, but the relief of saying it made her feel like collapsing.

Cece nodded and said, "I think I should post an announcement saying that Brenna has been found, and thanking everyone for their thoughts, prayers, and help in searching. I'll write a statement and just copy and paste it on each account."

"Do you want some help?" Roger asked, leaning toward her. A lock of his hair fell forward, and he brushed it back. "Just tell me how you want it worded, and I can handle part of it."

Deborah watched as they worked together, their heads leaning over their respective tablets. Roger seemed like such a down-to-earth young man, and thoughtful too. He'd stayed the entire night to help, which was no small thing.

Once they'd finished, Cece said, "I hate to ask you to leave, Roger, but my sister will be home soon, and I think we just want family here."

As Cece walked him to the front door of the apartment, Deborah heard Roger suggesting different restaurants. "Or we could go back to that karaoke bar you liked."

"I'm not sure I'll be up for anything anytime soon," Cece said.

"Sure, I get it. I'll give you a few days," Roger said.

When Cece came back into the room, Deborah said, "He seems like a good guy."

"He is." She sank back onto the sofa and stretched out her legs. It had been a long night. "A very good guy, which is why it's going to be hard to tell him I just want to be friends."

Deborah ventured a guess. "Too needy?"

"No, it's not that. He's a lot of fun and smart too, but I real-ized tonight that we really don't have much in common. He loves classical music and baseball and playing chess and chicken wings, none of which appeals to me. And I love fashion and pop music and Broadway shows. He'll do whatever I want, but I don't want someone to just go along to make me happy. Plus, I'm going to be really busy with my new fashion line, so there's that." She yawned. "I can't wait to have Brenna home."

"That makes two of us." Deborah surveyed her elder daughter in amazement. She'd seen a different side of her tonight, so different from her public persona. This family crisis had spurred in her a take-charge attitude she'd never seen before. When Harry had first dreamt up the idea of Cece as a social media celebrity, he'd pitched it to her as an extension of Cece's own personality. "She's so fun-loving and feminine, all about her friends and her clothing and accoutrements. We'll have her be the front for a line of clothing. We can work with a lab to develop a scent that we'll market as her signature fragrance."

When Deborah had expressed doubts about putting Cece out in front of the public eye, he'd waved away her hesitations. "We'll give her the choice, of course, but she has no idea what she wants to do anyway, so why would she turn down an opportunity like this?" He painted a mental picture for her. "I see Cece as sort of a modern-day Marilyn Monroe. Glamorous and mysterious. She already has the soft, whispery voice, and she's a beauty, as beautiful as her mother." The compliment about her beauty was intended to sway her, and it did soften her stance a bit. She finally conceded his point. In the end, he talked Cece into it, and the venture had taken off in a big way. They'd measured Cece's success in the number of followers, likes, and promotional opportunities that came her way. What neither she nor Harry noticed was that the more Cece put herself out there, the more she receded personally. It was as if maintaining the public persona sucked all the life out of her, leaving nothing left for her actual real life.

Tonight she'd seen what her daughter was capable of, given the circumstances. She was, when given the chance, smart and strong and clever. Had she always been that way? Could it be that as well-meaning as they'd been, they'd somehow robbed her of the opportunity to be the star of her own life? Suddenly there was something she had to know. She said to Cece, "Can I ask you something?"

Cece looked up, curious. "Of course."

"The past few years—all the videos and photos and public appearances you did to build your social media presence. Did you enjoy any of it?"

Cece tilted her head to one side. "At first I did. Then it got tiresome. The worst part was not having any say in things."

Deborah nodded. "I wouldn't like that either."

"I'm glad I'm not doing that anymore."

CHAPTER 28

The front door of the Park Slope townhouse was opened by a man in his early thirties. He wore pajama bottoms and a white T-shirt, his hair tousled and face unshaven. He introduced himself as Colton Griffin and shook hands with Harry and the two police officers as they came through the door. Harry was no sooner in the entryway than Brenna came running down the stairs. When she reached the bottom, she barreled forward, throwing her arms around him. "Daddy!" She buried her face in the front of his shirt.

Daddy. She hadn't called him that in years, preferring to call him Dad, when she addressed him at all. His work and his travel kept him so busy, it didn't allow for much time at home. His connection to Brenna, he realized now, was almost nonexistent. He couldn't remember the last time they'd had a conversation or spent any time together, just the two of them. Wrapping his arms around her, he softly said, "Oh, Brenna. We were so worried."

"I'm sorry. I'm so sorry. I shouldn't have gone outside by myself." The words were muffled but heartbreakingly sincere.

"It's okay, Brenna. You're not in trouble. Don't cry, baby." He wanted to hold on to her and never let go. In his mind, this had been such a close call. He'd almost lost his daughter. He clutched her tight, wondering when she'd become such a big girl. It seemed like not that long ago she'd been a newborn, the tiniest little thing. Six pounds, two ounces. The idea to name her Brenna had been his. Deborah had wrinkled her brow when he mentioned it. "You mean Breanna?" she'd asked, and he'd said no, he meant Brenna. Two syllables. He liked the name. It was unusual but not too far out there. Feminine but not too girly. He didn't have to make much of a case for it—since his wife had picked Cecilia's name, he got his way.

Brenna.

Brenna gulped and said, "How come you want to fire Nanny? It's not fair."

"We're not firing Nanny. It was a misunderstanding. I'm sorry it upset you."

She sniffled, and then a woman came down the stairs, a toddler on her hip. She introduced herself as Callie and the little boy as Oliver, then ushered them all into the living room. "Would anyone like anything to drink—a cup of coffee, some water, a soft drink?"

"No, ma'am," said both of the cops. Harry took a pass as well. A small brown-and-white dog with pointed ears trotted in and sat down next to the couch.

The police officers, both young guys, said they wanted to ask Brenna what exactly had happened, and Harry sat next to her, his arm around her shoulders, while she answered their questions. It was a simple story. She'd gotten lost looking for Nanny's house. She'd been walking for hours when the Griffins' daughter, Summer, gestured for her to come inside, and she'd been there ever since. "I know not to go inside someone's house when I don't know them, but I saw the creepy man, and I wanted to get away from him," she said.

"That was a smart move," the first police officer said. "Good job."

His partner added, "By the way, we found the guy you called the creepy man. He won't be bothering you anymore, Brenna."

Harry nodded. He'd heard this already, but Brenna needed to know it as well. She didn't need the idea of a bogeyman lurking in every shadow.

"We saw the news footage about Brenna's disappearance last night, but we didn't know she was here until this morning," Callie said, almost apologetically. She set the little boy down on the floor, and he walked precariously over to his father, who scooped him onto his lap.

Harry said, "The important thing is that she's fine. Her mother and sister and I have been worried sick. I've been walking around looking for her for hours." He leaned over and kissed the top of Brenna's head, something he did naturally even as he was aware this kind of spontaneous affection was so unlike him. He was getting old, that's what it was. With one daughter grown and another on her way to adulthood, it was hitting him that life was finite. His loved ones weren't waiting in the wings for him to get around to spending time with them. The problem had been that he just hadn't been paying attention, and this was the outcome. Years had passed and his daughters had grown. He'd been completely preoccupied with business and had taken them for granted, and look where it had gotten him. Something terrible could have happened to Brenna, a little girl all alone and out in the world overnight. It was a stroke of luck that she landed someplace safe.

With a start, he realized that his prayer had been answered. He'd begged for the safe return of his daughter and had promised to become a better father and person in return. Harry was a man of business, one who dealt in facts and figures, cause and effect. Normally matters of the spiritual variety weren't intrinsic to his mindset. Would he have found his daughter safe and unharmed regardless of his plea to God? He couldn't say for certain. What he did know was that he'd prayed and his prayer had been answered. Cause and effect. He was a man of business, but he was also a man of integrity, priding himself on keeping his word. He'd made a promise, and he would keep it. It seemed the right thing to do.

After the police officers were done asking questions and taking notes, one of them said, "That about wraps it up. If we have any other questions, we'll be in touch."

"So I can take my daughter home now?" Harry asked.

"Yes, sir. We can give you a ride, unless you've made other arrangements."

He considered how long it would take for a car to arrive and then gratefully accepted. "I'll take you up on that offer. Thank you." He looked down at Brenna. "How about it? Want to ride in a police car with your old man?" As a boy he would have considered a ride in the back of a cop car such a thrill.

Brenna's eyebrows rose in surprise. "I'm not in trouble?"

"Not in trouble at all. The nice officers are just giving us a ride home."

A shy smile spread across her face. "Then I'd like that."

Harry shook hands with the young couple, thanking them again. "I'm lucky that my daughter wound up in your loving home. Tell Summer that I am very grateful to her." He glanced down at Brenna, who had crouched down next to him, cooing to the dog while rubbing behind his ears. Harry leaned in to quietly add, "Who knows what would have happened otherwise. I hate to even think about it. Your daughter is a hero in my book."

Brenna said, "Tell Summer I said goodbye."

Callie swallowed and nodded but didn't say a word.

When Harry and Brenna followed the police officers outside, he was startled by how light it had gotten. The night was turning to morning, almost as if the world knew his life was brighter now that he had his daughter back.

CHAPTER 29

*A*fter leading Harry to the townhouse, Dalton and Greta had said goodbye to him, allowing him to reunite with his daughter privately. A moment later, Greta's phone went off. She retrieved it from her bag and examined the screen. "It's Cece," she told him, right before turning it on and putting it on speakerphone.

When Cece gave them the good news, Greta said, "We know. We were with your dad when he got the call from your mom. We don't know the details, though. What happened?" As they listened silently, Cece spilled all of it, one incredible detail after another, ending with: "Isn't that crazy? The whole night she's been in some stranger's house, and the parents didn't even know she was there."

Greta said, "I'm so glad she's okay. What a relief."

Cece said, "After she and my dad get home, I'm giving her an enormous hug, and then I'm going to crash. This night has taken a lot out of me."

"Me too," Greta said. "But I've still got an adrenaline buzz. I think Dalton and I are going to get something to eat before we head back."

"Sounds good. See you later."

She put the phone back in her bag. "Such a relief to hear that Brenna's fine. I didn't want to say it out loud, but I was seriously worried. I wouldn't have said this to Cece, but anything could have happened to her. She could have been kidnapped or killed."

"And yet she wasn't." He gave her a soft smile.

"No, luckily she wasn't."

"So," he said, "you were thinking we would get something to eat?"

"I was thinking *I* was starving. I'm going out to breakfast regardless, but I would love it if you came along."

"Then I'll come along. Did you have someplace in mind?"

"I'm still new in town, so I'm open to ideas."

"I know this great blintz place, if you like that kind of thing."

Greta had an idea that blintzes were similar to crepes. Skinny, eggy pancakes. "Blintzes sound great."

They headed down the sidewalk together. As his fingers brushed against hers and then closed around her hand, her heart swelled with happiness. She was tired but still somehow energized by the night's emotional roller coaster. They'd been so wrapped up in worrying about Brenna that it was only now that she felt like she was spending time with Dalton, just the two of them heading out on what felt like a date. An unconventional date, seeing as it followed being part of a search party expedition, but a date all the same. "You know," she said, "that's a total New York thing to say."

"What's that?' His eyebrows rose.

"Saying things like *I know this great blintz place.*" She grinned. "People here are always saying things like that." She attempted a New York accent. "*I know this great gyro place. I know the best deli. I know this great steakhouse. You haven't lived until you've had the brick oven pizza. Nothing tops the cannoli at this great place I know.*"

He laughed. "People in Wisconsin don't know great places?"

"They do, but they aren't big on making proclamations. I

mean, what if I think it's great but you don't? It's risky making declarative statements like that."

"But that's not the right way to think about it. You need to be more confident. If you know about something great, you shouldn't hold back. Just own it."

"Own it?" She thought it over.

"Well, yeah. If you think it's great, chances are someone else will too. You're doing them a favor by sharing your opinion."

"I'll keep that in mind."

When they got to the end of the block, they turned off a residential street onto a stretch lined with neighborhood stores. The street was quiet. No pedestrians and only light traffic. Most of the stores hadn't opened for the day's business. As they approached a darkened storefront, Dalton suddenly pulled her into the entryway into an embrace, and before she could say a word, his mouth lowered to meet hers, hesitating for just a moment until she accepted the invitation. For the next few minutes, Greta wasn't sure where she ended and he began. She was aware of the morning breeze and the honking of a car horn off in the distance, but it all seemed so inconsequential, so trivial compared to the two of them together.

When he pulled away, he said, "Just so you know, I've been waiting to do that all night. It didn't seem appropriate with your cousin missing."

She nodded, her heart full. "I know."

"Was that okay? I don't want to be pushy. Tell me what you're thinking."

"I'm thinking"—she gave him a mischievous grin—"*that I know this great guy. You haven't lived until you've met him. He's just the best.*"

He whistled and shook his head appreciatively. "You are really something, you know that, Greta?"

"Well, you said if I knew about something great, I shouldn't hold back." She tapped the side of her head. "See, I listen! I was taking notes."

He kissed her again, and this time she let herself relax into his arms.

They would have continued this way indefinitely, Dalton with his back against the door, Greta pressed up against him, except for a man's loud throat clearing right behind them. She hadn't heard him walk up, so she turned, startled to see an older man about her height holding up a ring of keys. "Excuse me," he said. "I need to open the store?"

Greta felt the heat of embarrassment as it rose to her cheeks. "Sorry." Together she and Dalton moved away from the door, which she now noticed was the entrance to an upscale kitchen supply store.

Dalton said, "Sorry, dude," but judging from the slight smirk on his face, he wasn't even the least bit apologetic.

The man sighed while fumbling the key into the lock. "Not a problem. I just have to get inside." The key clicked in the lock, and he pushed the door open and went in. As they stood there, the lights went on, one row at a time.

"Well, unless you need an egg timer or wine opener, I guess we should be on our way," Dalton said, taking her hand and continuing down the sidewalk. "It's up to you. Should we get a ride or walk over the bridge?"

Greta tapped her chin with one finger. "Huh, what to do? What a conundrum. We've been walking for hours, so I guess my choice is collapsing from exhaustion and dying on the bridge or getting a ride and eating blintzes. I vote for the ride."

* * *

THE BLINTZES HAD JUST BEEN SERVED when Dalton asked about her future. "So," he said carefully, "I know you're here for the summer. Any chance you might stay on after that?" He leaned an elbow on the table while studying her face.

"Funny you should mention it." She took a sip from her coffee cup. "Cece is determined to make me stay. She's offered me a permanent job."

"Really." He sat back, his smile widening. "What sort of job?"

"Well, as you know already, she's breaking free from her previous schedule and wants to call all the shots now. She wants to design her own clothes, but she didn't seem to realize that she had signed contracts that keep her locked into doing the things her dad arranged for her and her company. She has to either get out of the contracts or see them through. After I told her this, she put me in charge of dealing with the paperwork and figuring out all the legalities."

"Kind of a big responsibility."

"I'll say. She says she doesn't do details." Greta focused her attention on her plate and took a bite of her blintz. "Oh my, this is heaven. This is the best-tasting thing I've ever had in my life."

"See? I told you I knew a great blintz place."

"I will never doubt you again."

They ate silently, while around them the restaurant hummed with conversation and the clinking of silverware on plates. When the young woman who'd served them came to check on their first bites, Dalton gave her a thumbs-up and said, "Superb as usual."

"That's what we like to hear."

Once the server had moved on to the next table, Greta said, "So it looks like I'm staying in New York for the foreseeable future. I thought my parents would be upset, but I ran the possibility past them, and they seemed fine with it." She lifted her shoulders. "They're glad I have a job and feel good about me living in an apartment in the same building as the Vanderhavens. My folks are talking about visiting before the summer is over."

"Did you tell them about me?"

"I did."

His mouth curved into a smile, and his eyes widened, prompting her. "And?"

"You want to know what I said about you?" She tilted her head to one side, a teasing grin widening.

"Yes, I do. If it's not too personal."

Greta had never been one to give away her heart too easily. Sometimes the heady feeling of a new infatuation felt like being in a plane taxiing down a runway. Liftoff seemed imminent but not guaranteed, and talking about it seemed like a good way to jinx the whole thing from progressing any further. Still, this time felt different. She and Dalton had an immediate connection, and it hadn't faded in the days since she'd met him. He was proving to be the man she'd thought he was—funny, smart, kind, and caring. Of course, that described a lot of people, but in this case, his version of those traits clicked with her own personality. Spending time with him, hearing his voice, feeling his hand in hers touched a place deep in her heart. Oh, she would be devastated to find out she'd been wrong about him, but she didn't think she was. "I told them that I met this great guy named Dalton Bishop and we totally hit it off."

The emotion that flickered in his eyes was hard to discern. "And that's it? Nothing else?"

She took in a deep breath. "Oh, they had questions about your background and your family. You know, the usual. How old is he? What does he do for a living? What does he look like?"

"And you said?"

"I said you were homeless when I met you, but now, after only a few days of knowing me, you're heading up a charitable foundation for a major corporation. I saw your potential right from the start." She tapped her chin with her fingertips. "Oh, and that you used to look kind of scruffy, but you've cleaned up very nicely. I do believe I'm an excellent influence."

He laughed, one hand flat against the table. "And here I thought you were this shy girl from Wisconsin. Now you're all cocky and taking credit for my accomplishments."

"Well, maybe you're a good influence on me as well."

Once they were done with the blintzes, they took a refill on their coffee, and Greta resumed the conversation about her new job.

"The thing is," she said, "I'm excited about being part of Cece's new vision for her company. In a way, it's like coming on board a start-up. The only problem is that she seems to feel I can understand the contracts, and that's not exactly my area of expertise. I start to read them and realize I'm definitely in over my head, and I worry that I'll let her down."

"That's what attorneys are for." Dalton spoke with the surety of someone who'd encountered this kind of thing before. "The Vanderhaven Corporation is sure to have legal counsel in-house. Make an appointment to go see them, and take Cece with you. Have them explain what the contracts mean in terms of her legal obligations. Even if she doesn't do details, she needs to know what's going on."

She gave him an appreciative nod. "Thanks. That helps."

"So what's your title at this new job?"

"Cece said I can have any title I want. She also told me to pick a salary and set up my own benefits. Plus, I'm living in her apartment for free."

His jaw dropped. "She told you to choose your own salary?"

"Yes. She said she trusts me to be honest and make it fair. And I will, of course." If anything, Greta had planned to keep her salary on the low side. Because she wasn't having to pay for rent, her expenses would be reasonable.

Dalton shook his head in disbelief. "Someone needs to watch out for that girl and make sure she's not taken advantage of."

"I guess that's going to be my job." Greta took another sip of her coffee. Most of the time venturing outside her comfort zone terrified her, but with Dalton as a resource, she thought she could handle this.

"She's lucky to have you." A look of pride crossed his handsome face.

"I would say I'm the lucky one." Seeing his smile and the love in his eyes, Greta couldn't help but think her chance at a happy future had never been brighter.

CHAPTER 30

When they were just a few blocks away, Harry texted Deborah to let her know he and Brenna were on their way. Deborah called down to the lobby to let the staff know. "My husband and daughter will be arriving in a police car in a few minutes, so if you could make sure they get a clear path to the elevator, we would appreciate it," she said, looking down through the living room window. She was too high up to see much of anything, unfortunately. "Yes, this is good news. Please thank everyone for all their help. Harry and I are very grateful." After hanging up, she felt at loose ends; it was so hard to wait. She fought the urge to come down in the elevator and meet them in the lobby. So much of their life was public. Some things were best left personal.

But she was ready when they came through the door. She folded Brenna into a warm embrace. Upon hearing their voices, Cece came running in from the kitchen and turned it into a group hug.

"Did anyone hurt you?" Deborah asked, her hands on either side of her daughter's face. She inspected Brenna from head to toe. She wore yesterday's clothes, which were rumpled, but her hair was sleek and her face clean. Her smile was reassuring as well.

"No." She shook her head.

Deborah looked into her eyes. "You were safe the whole time? No one did anything to you?" Harry had told her as much, and the police had questioned Brenna and found her to be fine, but she still felt compelled to ask. She needed the reassurance.

"No one did anything to me. I was just lost, and I couldn't find my way home."

Deborah asked, "But why did you just leave? Why didn't you at least talk to us first?"

"I don't know. I just . . . I don't know why." She sounded so forlorn, Deborah was sorry to have pushed the issue. Brenna swallowed and said, "I just wanted to talk to Nanny, and then I got lost going to her house."

"Well, you're home now," Cece said. "Nothing bad can happen to you here."

"It's good to be home," Harry said, sounding like he really meant it. He surveyed the three of them while running a hand through his unruly hair. Usually this kind of statement was followed by a comment about having to check work emails or make phone calls in his home office. Even when he was with them, his attention was elsewhere. Their yearly month-long trips to Paris forced him to spend one-on-one time with Deborah, but even then, he managed to stay connected to business. The only change was that he had to make allowances for the time difference when scheduling phone conferences. Now, though, he stood and watched his family like a man taking the measure of his life and liking what he saw.

Brenna was still small enough to have her mother rest her chin on top of her head. "Oh, Brenna," she murmured.

"I missed you, baby girl." Cece rubbed her little sister's back. "Let's not do this again."

Mentally, Deborah did a family head count, relief and happiness washing over her in knowing that the four of them were here together. Having her younger daughter back felt like all of them had dodged a bullet. Despite all of Cece's efforts to keep her busy and distracted, in her head she'd played out all kinds of horrible scenarios. She'd tried not to think the worst, but it was hopeless. Every television episode or movie involving kidnapping or child abduction had spooled in her brain, with Brenna a substitute for the child actor. The worst part was not knowing where she was.

She was here now, and their family was whole again. That's all that mattered.

"I'm sorry, Mom. I'm so sorry." Brenna sounded on the verge of crying.

"I know, honey." Deborah stroked her hair. "You don't have to apologize. We're not angry. Just talk to us next time."

"I will." She looked up, her eyes glistening, and met her mom's gaze. "I promise."

"Are you hungry, honey? I can have Cook make you something to eat."

Brenna nodded. "I am kind of hungry. Tired too, but first of all I'm hungry." She rubbed her eyes with her fist, the way she used to when she was a tiny girl.

"Come with me," Cece said. "Cook's not here yet. I can make you a sandwich. Or maybe a bowl of cereal?"

Cece's repertoire of food preparation had its limits. Maybe, Deborah thought, now that her daughter was living with Greta, she might learn a thing or two. She couldn't imagine that Greta, having grown up in a middle-class family in her home state, hadn't learned at least how to cook the basics. A good hamburger, baked chicken, some broiled fish. Lasagna with a big salad and garlic bread. Homemade bean soup. A long time ago, she herself knew how to cook those things and more. Maybe one of these days she'd surprise Harry and Brenna and cook dinner for the three of them. Deborah said, "You girls go ahead. I just need to talk to your father for a minute, and then we'll be right in to join you."

Cece draped her arm around her sister's shoulder and the two of them walked slowly toward the kitchen. All of them had missed a night's sleep, and the fatigue was now catching up to them.

Harry followed Deborah into the living room and sank into one of the chairs. "I could fall asleep right here," he said. "I think it's emotional as much as it is physical. I feel like I had all this worry and fear building and building, and then once we found her, all my worries left, but it sapped my energy along with it."

"I know what you mean." Deborah sat forward in her chair, resting her elbows on her knees. "I'm spent. I think all of us need some sleep."

Harry gave her a knowing look. "You wanted to talk to me?"

"Yes. I know you told me about what happened with Brenna, but was there more? Something you couldn't say over the phone?" She wanted to know, even as she was afraid to know. Harry had said the guy Brenna called "the creepy man" hadn't touched her and hadn't said anything menacing, but she wanted confirmation once again, for her own peace of mind.

"No, I told you everything."

"So the man who tried to extort money from us—he never got close to her?"

"Well, close enough, but nothing happened," he said. "She said the first time she saw him he sat next to her on the subway and was leaning in to talk to her. She must have looked uncomfortable, because a young woman told him off and told Brenna he should move to another seat. That's when she sat next to Gilda. Later, she saw him twice in Park Slope. The first time he pretended it was a coincidence, and the next time he said her name and it scared her, so she took off. Right after that, she went into the Griffins' house." He sighed audibly. "I can't even imagine what was going through her mind." There was a heart-breaking sadness in his voice.

Off in the kitchen, Deborah heard Brenna laugh. Cece must have done something silly to amuse her sister. She kept her attention on her husband and said, "I'm glad you didn't take her to task for leaving the house without permission. I thought you might overreact."

Harry didn't speak for a minute or so, and the look on his face became thoughtful. Finally, he said, "I do have a tendency to do that, don't I? Overreact, I mean."

Deborah said, "I didn't mean to sound critical."

"I know. You've always been patient with me. Your father was right: I was lucky to wind up with you. No one could have been a better wife to me." She started to speak, and he held up a hand. "If you could just hold that thought, I have something really important to say."

"Of course."

"I had a lot of time to think when I was walking around showing people Brenna's picture." He tented his fingers together and thought of how best to explain his epiphany. Having time to think was just the start of it. Having to ask strangers if they'd seen his daughter had brought him out of his life in a surreal sort of way. While he'd walked the streets, odd thoughts had flashed through his mind, a kind of movie montage of his life, and he realized that most of it involved his work life, which was so all-consuming that his memories of his family were almost a footnote. He'd always justified his time away from Deborah and his daughters. The girls had done fine in his absence. Deborah understood. His income provided them with a fabulous lifestyle. On those occasions when he missed a big event—a recital, a school play, a birthday—he'd always made up for it with an expensive gift. Upon reflection, it was possible that the fact that he had daughters rather than sons made spending time with them seem less essential. They had female role models galore: Deborah, Margaret, and their teachers and tutors.

Would it have been different if he'd had boys? He was forced to acknowledge that this might be the case. So he was an absentee father and unwittingly sexist as well. What a mess he'd made of his home life.

"You had a lot of time to think . . . ," Deborah prompted.

"Yes. When I wasn't worrying, I was thinking about my family. *Our* family." He met her gaze, and she caught the regret in his eyes. "The years have gone by so fast, and I have missed so much. It's too late for Cece. She's already grown up and off on her own, but I still have time with Brenna." He leaned forward, lacing his hands together and watching for her reaction. "I'd like to make a change."

"So what are you proposing to do differently?"

"Everything. Mark my words, things are going to be different from now on. I'm going to make you and the girls my top priority. No matter what."

Harry's tone was so sincere that Deborah wanted to believe him. She said, "I know you mean it, but we've had this conversation before, and I don't have to tell you how it goes." So many times she'd begged him to at least come home for dinner by six. Even if he had to go back to work afterward, dinner seemed a reasonable request. He'd always agreed. Sometimes he even managed two or three days in a row before things went back to the way they'd always been. There was always a good reason—a critical juncture in a merger, a major tax crisis, an international shipment stuck in some distant port. Emergencies popped up at every turn.

His eyes stayed on her for several more seconds before he said, "It's going to be different this time."

"You sound awfully certain."

"I *am* certain." He nodded confidently. "This time it's going to stick. It has to—I made a promise."

CHAPTER 31

*S*cott arrived home from work to find Lauren sitting at the kitchen table, her back straight, the day's mail next to her elbow. She'd been reading from a piece of paper but stopped and looked up as he walked in. He gave her a quick kiss. "What do you have there?"

Her eyes narrowed with what he knew was irritation. "A letter from Callie. Can you imagine that? My own sister has so much trouble talking to me that she sat down and wrote a letter, folded it up, put a stamp on it, and mailed it to me."

He pulled up a chair and sat. "What does it say?"

"See for yourself." She slid it over to him, then leaned back and crossed her arms.

Scott began to read. "Dear Lauren."

"No, don't read it out loud." She frowned. "I don't want to hear it."

He nodded and read it to himself. He couldn't help but hear his sister-in-law's voice behind the words.

Dear Lauren,

I know that things between us have been strained for the last few years, and I can't tell you how sorry I am for pushing you away. I take full responsibility for that. We used to be so close. I really miss you.

When Summer died, I was devastated. I know I lashed out at you, and you didn't deserve it. And then later, I was going through so much that I couldn't talk about because I was grieving too much to even articulate it.

The pain was unbearable. I wondered why God would give me a beautiful, perfect little girl only to take her away. Why did this happen to me and Colton? We were good people and loving parents. I read about people who abused their kids, and none of it made sense. Why did they get what I couldn't have? It was so unfair. I was angry at God for a long, long time.

Eventually, I got tired of being so miserable and depressed. That's when I went to see the grief counselor I told you about. Bit by bit, she was able to help me. I still have my difficult days, but I've also found I can now think about my daughter and remember happy times.

The next step, for me, is to repair my relationship with you. I have so much to tell you, and I would love it if you would open up to me too. Right now I feel like there's a wall between us.

I hope you don't mind, but I've taken the liberty of making an appointment for a day spa visit for the two of us, a week from Saturday. Remember when we used to talk about doing that? I thought it would be a good environment for us to talk without being interrupted. You'll be getting an email with the details. I hope you will come.

Love,

Callie

Scott set the letter flat on the table and met her eyes. "I don't know why you're upset. This seems nice."

"Of course it seems nice." She grimaced. "Try reading between the lines."

"She said she was sorry, and she ended it by saying 'Love, Callie.'"

Lauren picked up the letter and surveyed the writing. "She says she's sorry for pushing me away. Notice that it's not an apology." Over the top of the page, her eyes shot daggers in his direction. She still remembered what Callie had said to her while the paramedics worked on Summer's lifeless body. After a few minutes, they'd directed them out of the bedroom into the hallway. The two of them had waited together, fearful and horror-stricken.

After thirty minutes, one of the paramedics, a young woman with her hair pulled back into a severe bun, had told them she was very sorry. "We've done everything we can, and she's still unresponsive, so we're calling it."

"Calling it?" Lauren couldn't even fathom what that meant.

"Calling the time of death." The woman had tears in her eyes. "I am very sorry. We did everything we could." And then she'd turned and gone back into the bedroom to join her colleagues.

It was then that Callie had lashed out at Lauren, saying the words that cut her to the bone. "You know Summer never takes a nap. You should have checked on her! Were you even paying attention, or were you on your phone the whole time?"

And when Lauren, sobbing, asked if she was blaming her, she'd said, "You better believe I'm blaming you. If you weren't so careless, my daughter might still be alive."

Thinking about it now made her sick.

None of it was true, of course. They found out later that Summer's heart had just stopped beating. A defect she'd had from birth. It could have happened anywhere, at any time. It just happened to be on Lauren's watch.

Later, she'd tried to talk to her sister, but all Callie had to say was, "I'm sorry if I overreacted. I was upset."

Overreacted. Upset. Minor words for a major assault. Lauren didn't think she was being petty for wanting more.

She returned to the page. "Signing it 'Love, Callie' is just sort of a generic sendoff. Nowadays people are doing that to most everyone. Love, love, love. Except for business, everyone signs everything with *love.*"

"I don't."

She disregarded what he'd said and carried on. "And notice that it's all about her. She was in pain. She was miserable. She went to a grief counselor. On and on all about Callie. She's not the only one who lost Summer, you know. All of us miss her."

Scott leaned his elbows on the table. "I see your point," he said slowly. "But I think Callie's really making an effort here. She said she misses you and wants to repair your relationship."

Lauren set the letter down. "And that's another thing. She says that's the next step for her, like I'm on a list of things to do. Probably her therapist's idea. Making amends as part of the healing process. Besides,"—her voice was harsh—"what gall to arrange a spa day and automatically assume I'd go. Even if she knew I was agreeable, which I'm not, how does she even know if I'm available? It's like she thinks I'm sitting around waiting for her to snap her fingers and I'll come running."

He tried to soften her mood. "But you are available. I mean, there's nothing on the calendar."

As he spoke, realization crossed her face. "You've got to be kidding me!" Her mouth dropped open, and she pressed the flat of her hand against the table. "You knew about this, didn't you? Callie called and asked if I was free for a spa day, and you said yes. My own husband was talking about me behind my back."

He held up a defensive hand. "It's not like that, Lauren. She didn't say anything about a spa day. She just said she had some-thing planned and wanted to know if you were available. I wasn't sure if she was sending a package or inviting you to lunch or what."

"But she asked you not to say anything to me," she said with certainty.

He lifted his shoulders and held out his hands like he was offering her something. "It was supposed to be a surprise. I didn't want to ruin it."

"Oh great, a surprise. What a surprise." She wiped away a

stray tear and looked past him to the window. "My own husband. And I thought we were a team, that you were on my side."

Scott winced. "Baby, I am on your side. I was just trying to help."

"Some help." Her head was down now, her gaze on her lap.

Scott decided that since she was mad at him already, it's not like anything he could say would make it any worse, so he decided just to come out with it. "I hate that you two are at odds. I mean, I used to be jealous of how close you were, but now I really miss it, and I miss how you used to be. You were happier then, and it's bleeding into the rest of your life. We have so few people in our lives who really know and love us. Life is short and getting shorter with every passing minute. Are you going to stay mad at her forever?"

She looked up, and now he saw tears streaming down her face. "I'm not mad at her." She wiped her cheeks with the back of her hand. "She's mad at me."

"That's not what it sounds like." He pointed to the letter. "Maybe she was before, but I don't think she is now. I think she's really trying." She didn't answer, so he said, "Don't you think this took some effort on her part?"

"I guess," she admitted reluctantly.

"So go and meet with her. See what she has to say." He rested a hand on her arm.

"It's not that easy, Scott. It's not like we had a disagreement and we can work it out. Summer died. I don't know how we move on from this."

"You never will if you don't try."

She got up from the table and sat on his lap, nestled into him while he wrapped his arms around her. "I don't think I can face Callie, just the two of us. It was bad enough going to the house for Oliver's birthday."

"Oh, Lauren. You can face her. You're the strongest, bravest, smartest woman I know. You can do it. I know you can."

She sighed and then was quiet, digesting his words. A minute later she said, "You seem so sure."

"I am sure. Besides, this will be a perfect opportunity to tell her our good news. She's going to find out sooner or later. Better now."

"I dread telling her." She looked up at him, her mouth twisting in a thoughtful way. "And I hate that I dread it."

"I know."

"I wish you were going to be there."

"You'll do fine. You're both making an effort. I think it will go well."

"But what if it doesn't? What if I'm in a bathrobe in the middle of a pedicure or something and she brings up that I should have checked on Summer that day and maybe I would have noticed something that would have saved her life and I start to cry and it all gets worse?" She took a very deep breath. "You know I wouldn't be able to deal with that."

"That won't happen." He rubbed her back in small, circular strokes. "She knows that's not true. The medical examiner said it happened instantly. No one could have saved her."

"If Callie says anything that sounds remotely critical, I know I'm going to lose it."

"If that happens, you can still leave. Just say you're not feeling well, get dressed, and come home to me. At least you'll know that you tried to patch things up and nothing more can be done. And I will be here to tell you I love you and I'm proud of you for making the effort."

She looked up at him, her eyes clear and filled with devotion. "I love you so much, Scott."

"I love you too." He pulled her into a tight embrace, and she melted into him. "So you'll go, then? You'll meet with Callie?"

"I'm not sure," she said. "I'll think about it."

CHAPTER 32

*L*auren's stomach churned as she pushed open the glass door stenciled with the words "New Serenity Life Spa." The lobby was modern, with black quartz tile floors and marble columns. Behind a boomerang-shaped desk sat two employees—a guy and a young woman, both good-looking enough to be models. A huge, brightly colored mandala hung on the wall behind them.

Ten days earlier, she'd called and left a message for Callie, agreeing to meet her at the spa on Saturday. When her sister had called back, she deliberately hadn't answered. She wasn't sure why she was so afraid of talking to her alone. Things had gotten so awkward between them since Summer died that Lauren had developed a tendency to avoid her sister, holding Scott as close as a life preserver at every family gathering.

Lauren knew that losing a child had been devastating for Callie, but she also knew she wasn't alone in her suffering. Lauren had lost her niece, the light of her life, and to be blamed for Summer's death had hurt her to the core. And then, the final blow, she'd lost a sister, her best friend, as well.

On her voice mail, Callie had just acknowledged her call and said she was looking forward to seeing her. It was almost too bad that the spa appointment was so many days away. It gave her an excessive amount of time for nervous fretting. What had Callie been thinking, scheduling their first one-on-one, in-depth conversation at a spa? Lunch would have been better. At least then she could have bolted if things got too difficult. At a spa, she'd be vulnerable and trapped.

Lauren approached the desk. "I'm meeting my sister here. She booked a spa day for the two of us."

"Certainly!" The young woman, whose nameplate identified her as Deidre, turned her attention to the monitor in front of her. "Name, please?"

"I think it would be under my sister's name. Callie Griffin?"

Deidre squinted. "Yes, we have your reservation. You have the day package with lunch at noon and one other chosen option, a facial or pedicure, scheduled at two thirty. Otherwise, you have the use of the lazy-river pool, the hot tub, the steam room, and our relaxation chamber."

Her coworker, Kyle, said, "You're going to love it!"

That remained to be seen. Lauren gave him a polite nod.

Deidre handed her a key attached to a stretchy spiral bracelet. "This goes to your locker. Feel free to help yourself to a bathrobe and flip-flops. I assume you brought a swimsuit?"

"Yes." She turned the key over in her hand. The number 27 was stamped on one side.

"Great!" Kyle said with a big grin. He pointed at Lauren. "At the end of the day, you're going to feel like a new person, believe me. All your stress and tension will just melt away."

Deidre handed her a brochure. "Just head through those doors." She gestured with a jerk of her chin. "First door on the right is the women's locker room. Your sister already checked in. You should be able to find her, but if you can't, ask a staff member for help."

Of course Callie would already be there. Promptness was

nonnegotiable with her. But why couldn't she have waited in the lobby? Going into the locker room by herself suddenly felt daunting. Lauren would have turned around and left right that minute if not for the promise she'd made to Scott. "Just go and listen to what she has to say. And then speak your own truth because she needs to know how you feel as well," he'd said. "Can you do that?"

She'd promised she would stay at least long enough to listen to what Callie had to say, although she was sure she already knew what it would be. Another apology for her initial outburst, along with a plea for things to be back the way they had been, once upon a time. Friends again. It sounded good in theory, but in practice? Not so much. Callie's blame still hung out there, casting a shadow over her. And to make it worse, the pain of losing Summer was amplified when they were together. Her death was the final common bond they shared, a pain that overrode a lifetime of good memories.

"That's it, then?" Lauren asked.

"You're all set," Kyle said cheerily. "Enjoy!"

She tucked the brochure into her purse and headed for the door. She heard the buzz of the door release right before she turned the knob. On the other side, she found herself in a tiled hallway punctuated with the light smell of lavender. The women's locker room was, as she'd been told, on her right. She went in and found herself alone. As she looked around, another woman came out of a curtained cubicle wearing a white bathrobe with flip-flops on her feet; she shuffled past Lauren to get to the door.

Within a few minutes, Lauren had changed and locked up her possessions. With the key around her wrist, she traipsed out of the locker room, the backs of her footwear slapping against the bottom of her heels as she headed toward the sound of rushing water.

Behind glass doors she spotted the pool area, a rectangular

pool with an island in the middle. An unoccupied circular hot tub in the corner of the room bubbled with froth. A white-haired couple floated at one end of the pool, while two other women held on to foam noodles and floated on a circular current on the opposite side. Her sister stood on the deck, chatting with a curly-haired woman with a whistle draped around her neck.

Spotting Lauren's entrance, Callie broke from her conversation and her face lit up. She waved and came over to greet her. "I'm so glad you're here. I wasn't sure you would make it."

"Did you think I wouldn't be here? I said I would." That came out more defensively than Lauren intended. Quickly doing damage control, she said, "Thanks for inviting me. This place is great!" She kept her gaze on the lazy-river pool. "So the current carries you around in circles, I would guess?"

"Pretty cool, right? You want to try it?"

On either side of the pool were rows of lounge chairs. Callie led her to them, then draped her robe across one, kicking off her flip-flops. Lauren followed suit. After they each grabbed a noodle, they went down the steps into the pool. The woman Callie had been talking to said, "I'm glad you found your sister!" She leaned over the edge of the pool, and Lauren saw now that her polo shirt had the spa's logo on it. "You two look so much alike, you're practically twins."

Floating around in circles, Lauren felt herself relax. Maybe Scott was right—she'd worried too much. Next to her Callie sighed. "I needed this," she said, leaning forward onto the noodle. "It's been so hectic lately."

"Oliver seems like he's a handful," Lauren said. Immediately she realized her mistake in making a comparison. Summer had been such an easy baby and toddler. Poor Oliver could never compare in that area. "In a good way, I mean."

Callie didn't take it as a criticism. "You've got that right. If I could just borrow some of his energy, I could get so much done.

He just goes and keeps going, but when he's tired, he falls asleep so fast it's crazy. Like when a hypnotist snaps his fingers, you know? One minute he's playing, the next he's over on his side sleeping."

"Too funny."

They floated around the circumference of the pool and around again, just letting the flow of water carry them. Kyle had been right, Lauren reflected. She did feel all her stress and tension melting away.

Callie held on to the end of Lauren's noodle so they were in sync. "You didn't stay very long at Oliver's party."

"I know. I'm sorry."

"Why did you leave so early?"

"I don't know." She exhaled. "There were so many people there, and I just sort of felt out of place and overwhelmed." Too late she realized that this was not the excuse they'd given at the time.

"Hmm." Callie's mouth twisted to one side. "And that's it? You didn't leave because of something I said?"

"No, it was nothing you said."

Callie pointed to Lauren and back to herself. "You and me, we're okay, right? Because I feel like you're always avoiding me."

"Maybe I am a little bit." Lauren looked past her sister at the two other women who had now anchored themselves to the side of the pool and were deep in conversation. "It's hard for me to be around you and Colton."

"But why?"

The genuine concern in her voice touched Lauren's heart. Maybe she could speak her truth after all. She took a deep breath and said, "Because you blame me for Summer's death."

"I don't blame you!" Callie pulled herself up on the foam noodle to get a closer look at Lauren. "They said it was no one's fault. A heart abnormality. You knew that, right?"

Lauren nodded. "Still," she said, "you blamed me for what

happened. You said if I hadn't been so careless, Summer would still be alive." Three years later and the words still stung.

"No." Callie's face fell. "When did I say that?"

"That afternoon." Both of them knew which afternoon she meant. "I know you were upset, but afterward, when you knew the truth, you never took it back. Every time I see you now, I feel like you're judging me, and I can't stand the guilt and the shame and the sadness. It just comes over me, and I can't stand it."

Callie reached out to pat her arm. "Oh, Lauren, I am so sorry. I can't believe you've been carrying this around with you. I don't remember saying that at all. I don't doubt I said it, but you have to know I don't blame you. It was no one's fault." She shook her head. "I blanked out so much during that time. I have only vague memories of the funeral too. I looked at the guest book later, and there were names of people I had to have talked to, but it was such a blur I couldn't tell you if I saw them or not."

Lauren nodded. "It was all so horrible." She ran her hand through the water, watching as it created a small ripple. "So horrible." She turned and met her sister's eyes. "It wasn't supposed to be this way. She was so little and full of life. I still can't believe she's gone." She blinked back the start of tears. "The hardest part is that I was the last one to see her, so I feel like I robbed you of that."

"Oh, Lauren. No, no, no." She shook her head slowly. The older couple were now climbing up the stairs, pulling themselves up by the handrail to leave the pool. "I don't want you to feel bad about that."

"I know." She ran her hand through the water and lifted it, watching the drips coming off her fingertips. "I try not to feel bad about that, but I can't seem to shake the feeling."

Callie sighed. "I don't profess to have all the answers, but I can tell you that going for counseling has helped me a lot. My therapist said that one day I would be able to remember

Summer and instead of it making me miserable, I'd find myself smiling. I really doubted I'd ever get to that place, but one day, it happened. I'm not over her death. I don't know if I ever will be. I still miss her so much. There are moments where the grief catches me off guard and it almost takes my breath away, but for the most part it doesn't seem so pervasive anymore. And now with Oliver, we have so much to look forward to."

The question that had been weighing on Lauren's mind came out. "Do you ever worry that Oliver . . ." She couldn't manage to finish.

Callie blinked. "Has the same heart defect?"

"Yes."

"Oh, no. Oliver was checked a long time ago. His heart is perfectly healthy. You didn't know that?"

"No, I didn't know." Hearing this eased her mind. She had wanted to ask so many times but had been afraid to bring up the subject. "I'm so glad."

Callie let go of the noodle and pointed her thumb toward the corner of the room. "Do you want to go in the hot tub? There's something kind of important I wanted to tell you."

The hot tub was not an option for Lauren. "I'm not really in the mood for the hot tub. You want to sit in the lounge chairs instead?"

"Sure."

They climbed out of the pool and found a towel rack by the door. They dried off before putting on their robes and sitting down. Lauren sat with her legs outstretched in front of her, while Callie swung her legs to the side, facing her sister. "Something incredible happened," she said, her eyes alight with excitement. "I wanted to tell you about it right after it happened, but I didn't want it to be over the phone. I had to tell you in person. What happened is unbelievable. It's astounding. In a good way."

"Tell me."

"Do you remember when Brenna Vanderhaven went missing overnight?"

"Like two weeks ago? Sure, it was everywhere in the news."

"It actually happened the night of Oliver's party."

Lauren's eyes narrowed as she reflected. "Oh yeah, I guess it was."

"Do you know where she was found?" Callie's eyes widened.

She shook her head. "They never said, did they? Just that she had been safe the whole time and was once again home with her family. I assumed she'd been at a friend's house."

"No."

"No?"

"No." Callie leaned over, her elbows on her knees. "She wasn't at a friend's house. She was at *our* house. I found her in the morning sleeping in Summer's bed."

"What?" Lauren sat up straight. "How did that happen?"

"She was there the whole time, even during the party. Colton and I had no idea she was upstairs. We put Oliver to bed and cleaned up, then went to sleep. And then something incredible happened. I swear to you this is true. I had what I thought was a dream. I dreamed that Summer came into our bedroom. She put her hand on my face and kissed my cheek. I heard her voice saying, 'Mommy.' It was so real; I would have sworn she was there. And then right after that Baxter woke me up, and I got up to let him out, but instead of going down the stairs he went right to Summer's room, and that's when I found Brenna."

"How did she even get into your house?"

"This is the part that gets me teary every time I think about it. Brenna said she got lost trying to go to her nanny's house, and this creepy man she saw on the subway was following her. She saw the party guests going into our house, and when she looked up she saw Summer in the window upstairs. Summer motioned for her to come in."

"No." Lauren felt her chest constrict and her heart accelerate. "She saw Summer?"

Callie nodded emphatically. "She said when she came inside Summer motioned for her to come upstairs to her room. She told Brenna not to bother us during the party, and then Brenna fell asleep on her bed waiting."

"Did you believe her?"

Callie tilted her head and nodded. "I did."

"Did you ask her what Summer looked like?"

"Of course I did. I asked so many questions, and I would have asked more except Brenna was upset and wanted to go home."

"So what did Brenna say about Summer?"

"She said Summer looked like a regular little girl, just like the picture on her dresser. She described what she was wearing, and it was exactly what she had on the day she died. How would Brenna know that?"

Lauren's jaw went slack. "I don't know."

"Colton and I were so stunned we didn't know what to say. But she knew so much about our family and about Summer. How else would she know? And why would she lie? Brenna was already upset about getting lost, and she really wanted to go home. We didn't have the heart to tell her Summer was dead. The way Brenna talked, she'd just spoken to her. Both of us believe it."

The revelation was shocking and nearly impossible to come to terms with, but Lauren knew Callie wouldn't lie, especially about something this important.

Callie continued. "One of the things Summer told Brenna was that it made her sad that her mom and her aunt weren't friends anymore." She gave her a sad smile. "That's the main reason I reached out to you again. I figured if that's what Summer wants . . ."

"So you both really believe this little girl saw and talked to

Summer?"

"I *know* she did," Callie said emphatically. "I've been praying for a sign for so long. Grief counseling has helped heal me emotionally, but spiritually, I had to know that Summer was happy and at peace. I've been looking for signs for the longest time, but nothing happened until now." An expression of peaceful satisfaction came over her face.

Lauren stared at her, unsure what to think. Callie went on, talking about online message boards she frequented and how some of the members had received proof of their loved one's existence after they crossed over. She cited things like rainbows and feathers and dimes found in unlikely places. Some of them swore by certain psychic mediums who had communicated things no one outside of the family could have known, and others had dreams that felt more like visitations.

When she paused, Lauren said, "I'm not saying it wasn't Summer, but I have to be honest and tell you I'm having trouble wrapping my brain around this whole story."

"It's not a *story*," Callie said, making finger quotes around the last word. "I'm telling you what happened."

Lauren thought carefully before speaking. "I believe what you're saying, but just playing devil's advocate here, what if this is a publicity stunt created by the Vanderhavens? They could have found out things about your family online, or found out what Summer was wearing from medical reports and then planted Brenna in your house to say just the right things that would convince you she'd seen Summer." Lauren knew the Vanderhavens had enough money to find out anything. No information was off-limits if you were willing to pay for it.

Callie pursed her lips. "But why would they do that?"

"To draw attention to themselves? To generate publicity for their whole Vanderhaven empire? You have to admit, it makes for a great story."

Callie shook her head. "But you said yourself that they were very guarded about Brenna's whereabouts. And if you had seen Brenna, you would have known she wasn't acting. She couldn't possibly have been. She talked about Summer like she had been there, talking to her. To her, Summer was a real little girl. And when her father came to pick her up, he was so relieved he was practically crying. I don't believe any parent would put their eight-year-old child through this for publicity."

The silence between them was a wall. Finally, Lauren said, "I didn't mean to doubt you. I'm sure you can understand that this is a lot to digest."

"Of course." Callie sat back on the chair and stretched out her legs in front of her.

"For the record, I really want to believe it."

"Then believe it. I'm telling you it's true."

Lauren nodded. "Then that's good enough for me."

CHAPTER 33

cott was waiting when she arrived home. After giving her a hug, he said, "You made it! Lasted the whole day. Did you two work everything out?" He was hopeful, she could tell that much.

"Yes, we had a really good talk, and a lot was cleared up. I think we're going to be okay now."

He smiled. "I'm so glad for both of you."

"But that's not the half of it."

"There's more?"

"A lot more. Wait until I tell you." She hung her keys on the hook in the entryway and led him down the hall into the living room. Once they were both seated, she related Callie's story, starting with Oliver's birthday party and ending with Harry Vanderhaven coming to pick up his daughter. Her husband was quiet during the telling. He'd always been a good listener. Studying his face, she said, "So, what do you think?"

He shrugged. "That's pretty crazy."

"Right? What do you make of it?"

"I wasn't there, but it sounds like Callie and Colton believe Brenna actually talked to Summer."

"Not just talked to her. Saw her as if she were real. Not holographic or like a spirit in a movie. Solid, like she was when she was alive." Her tone was decidedly skeptical.

"It's a pretty incredible story," he admitted. "But anything is possible, I guess."

"Possible, but unlikely I think."

He nodded. "So how did you leave things? Does she know you're doubtful?"

"I basically said if she believes it, that's good enough for me. I sensed she wanted me to be more excited about it, but I just couldn't. I tried, honestly, but it was so far out there . . ."

"I see."

"I just hate to see Colton and Callie taken advantage of," Lauren said.

"How could they be taken advantage of?"

"What if the Vanderhavens are somehow behind this? Like, what if they're doing it as a publicity stunt? Cece has been the star of the show for years now. Maybe they're going to start some new show where Brenna is a psychic medium and does readings for celebrities or something. This could be an elaborate setup."

"Oh, babe." Understanding filled his eyes. "I like how you're looking out for your sister, but—and please take this the right way—I think you're getting ahead of yourself. Nothing has happened yet, and it seems unlikely that the Vanderhavens would even have the ability to stage this. In the meantime, if this brings Colton and Callie peace, I think it's a good thing. I would love to think that Summer saved a lost little girl from a potential kidnapper. She was such a sweetheart in life that it sounds completely in character for her to make friends with a child who was lost and afraid."

"I guess." She sighed. "That's not the end of it, though. The Vanderhavens are having some fancy reception at their apartment to thank Callie and Colton for finding Brenna, and she's invited me to come along as her guest. She said that Colton's staying behind to watch Oliver, and I'd go in his place." When her sister had asked, Lauren's heart had sunk. It was easy to read between the lines. Colton was staying behind because they didn't trust anyone to babysit for Oliver, not after what happened to Summer.

"Could be fun. Did you say you'd go?"

"Yeah, I said I would." She felt the need to explain. "I mean, I didn't want her to go alone, and you know we've been following Cece online for years."

"Believe me, I know." He grinned. So many times he'd shaken his head, not understanding the allure of watching videos of Cece and her friends. Of course, she'd never quite gotten his addiction to slasher films, which made them even.

"It's going to be very glamorous, which means I need to buy a new dress."

"And maybe some shoes and jewelry?" He said it kiddingly. Little did he know how true it was.

"If you insist." Now she was grinning. "I'll do it all—shoes, makeup, jewelry, handbag—the whole nine yards. This one's gonna cost."

"Those Vanderhavens." He shook his head. "They're going to bankrupt us."

"You've got that right."

He leaned back on the couch and put his feet up on the coffee table. "So I'm guessing you didn't tell Callie our news?"

"No, there was never a good opportunity."

"There's still plenty of time."

CHAPTER 34

*C*allie and Lauren went up the elevator to the Vanderhavens' together. The door was opened by a man Callie presumed was the Vanderhavens' butler. "Welcome. The Vanderhavens are so glad you could join them this evening." He didn't wait for them to answer, but turned his back and led them into the living room. The formality made Callie glad to have her sister with her.

When Cece had called to set up a convenient time, she'd made it sound casual. "Just my family and a few other friends to round things out," she'd said. "A simple evening at home." When Callie had thought to ask how they should dress, Cece answered, "However you like. This evening is a thank-you to you. We just want you to feel comfortable."

However you like. Thankfully Cece had also mentioned cocktails and hors d'oeuvres, giving the impression of a cocktail party. Callie and Lauren had dressed accordingly, and judging from the other guests, anything less would have been embarrassing. Both of them wore dark-colored cocktail dresses and high-heeled dress sandals. Dressing up had been the right call.

"Can you believe this place?" Lauren spoke from the side of her mouth.

"Amazing," Callie breathed.

They'd seen bits and pieces of Cece's parents' home in countless videos over the last few years. Callie had even made a point of replaying them in the previous week, pausing when the background was more visible to get a sense of where they would be going that evening. In the video footage, it was clear that this was an elegant, upscale home, but seeing it on a tiny screen didn't quite convey the grandeur. The ceilings, for one thing, soared high above them. Everything seemed more lavishly scaled. The furniture was oversize; the windows were floor-to-ceiling with thick drapes tied back with cords thick as tug-of-war ropes; the chandelier in the entryway was the size of a small car. For a second Callie wished she'd brought Colton along. He would have enjoyed seeing how the top one percent lived.

They walked into a room where a handful of guests socialized, all of them dressed for a formal reception. A man in a white button-up shirt sat at a grand piano, his sleeves rolled up to his elbows, his coat draped on the bench next to him. A beautiful young woman in a red strapless dress leaned on the piano and watched him play a classical piece, an admiring look on her face. At first glance, Callie thought the woman in red was Cece, but a moment later she saw the difference. It had to be Greta, the cousin who had been introduced recently on Cece's channel. The family resemblance was strong.

In one corner, Deborah and Harry Vanderhaven stood, talking animatedly to a young man who had a martini in one hand and a shoulder up against a bookcase. Brenna stood nearby, watching the adults. When Deborah spotted Callie and Lauren, she waved her hand in greeting, excused herself, and hurried over, with Brenna at her side. Callie was struck by her effortless elegance. She wore an off-the-shoulder plum-colored dress with a ruffled hemline, shorter in the front than the back. The low neckline emphasized the double-stranded diamond necklace that matched sparkling drop earrings.

Deborah was welcoming, exclaiming how happy she was that they were able to come. After they exchanged introductions, she hugged each of the sisters in turn. Turning to Callie, she said, "Callie, speaking to you from one mother to another, I have to tell you that the evening Brenna was gone was the longest and most awful night you can imagine. Knowing, even after the fact, that she was safe in your lovely home was the only positive in this whole dreadful experience."

"We were happy to help." Callie gave Brenna a smile.

"Brenna," her mother prompted. "Didn't you have something you were going to say to Callie?"

"Thank you for coming, Callie," Brenna said shyly, tugging at the front of her dress. "And for letting me stay in your house that night."

Callie said, "You're welcome, Brenna. Thank you for the invitation. We're glad to be here." She turned to give Deborah an explanation. "My husband is so sorry he couldn't make it. Our son, Oliver, has been teething the last week or so, and we didn't want to leave him with a sitter. You were so kind to let me bring my sister instead."

"We're delighted to have both of you here." Deborah smiled warmly. "I'm sorry your husband wasn't available, but it's perfectly understandable. And I was so looking forward to meeting Lauren." She was, Callie decided, the very definition of a well-mannered lady.

"Where's Summer?" Brenna asked. "I wanted to show her my room."

Callie took in a sharp breath and exchanged a glance with Lauren. They'd talked about this on the phone earlier in the week. Lauren felt Callie should tell her that Summer had died, but Callie, who had a mother's heart, did not see the point in upsetting Brenna. She swallowed and said, "Summer couldn't be here tonight."

"Of course. We understand." Deborah spoke with such certainty that for a second Callie thought maybe she'd investigated their family and knew the truth, but what she said next dispelled that notion. "A four-year-old would be way too young to stay up so late." She put her arm around her daughter's shoulders. "You're lucky we're letting you come to the party."

"You kind of have to," Brenna said, snuggling against her mother, "because I was the one who was lost."

"That is very true." Her mother kissed the top of her head. "Don't ever do that again."

In the corner of the room, the pianist had switched to playing a boogie-woogie version of the classical piece he'd been playing earlier, making the woman in the red dress laugh. "Oh, Dalton!" she cried out. The name Dalton put Callie in mind of the scene in Cece's video starring her cousin Greta singing karaoke with Dalton. Now that she'd assigned names to the faces, she found herself staring; Greta gave her a friendly wave.

"Let me introduce you to everyone," Deborah said, guiding them across the room. Along the way, they passed two men in white shirts and black vests. One held a tray of appetizers, the other a tray of champagne flutes. Deborah said, "You can just leave the trays of food on the sideboard." She gestured to a long piece of furniture against one wall.

Callie paused to take a drink off the tray. "Thank you."

Lauren said, "Is there some way I could get a glass of sparkling water?"

The waiter nodded and said, "Of course. I'll be right back with that."

They continued on, Deborah leading them to the corner of the room, where she introduced them to her husband, Harry, and another guy, a younger man named Roger who was, she said, a good friend of Cece's. "Roger was here the night that

Brenna was missing," she said. "He stayed all night manning the social media accounts with Cece. All night long. Now that's a true friend."

Roger blushed. "It was nothing. I'd do anything for Cece."

"Is Cece going to be here?" Callie asked, surveying the room.

"Any minute," Deborah assured her. "She just texted and said she was on her way up."

"Callie Griffin, it's nice to see you under better circumstances," Harry said, taking her free hand and holding it between his own. He was a tall man with a thick head of wavy dark hair threaded with silver. Callie couldn't help but think that like everything else in his home, he too was oversize. His wristwatch had a large face and thick band, and the cuffs of his sleeves were held together by nickel-size cufflinks—gold discs with diamonds in the center. "You and your family were my daughter's guardian angels that night. I can never thank you enough. I'm so glad you were able to join us tonight."

While the server handed Lauren her drink, Callie said, "Thank you for having us." They made small talk for a little while, Harry expressing interest in Lauren's marketing job and the commute to work each morning. Before long, Greta and Dalton had joined the group, introducing themselves and joining the conversation.

Dalton, they quickly learned, had a knack for putting people at ease. Within a few minutes, Callie and Lauren went from feeling like outsiders to being part of the group, talking about shows on Netflix and summer days in the park and the best places to go for brunch. "There it is again!" Greta exclaimed, nudging Dalton. "Right after I got to the city, I noticed that New Yorkers are constantly saying '*I know the best place . . .*' every time they recommend a restaurant. It's always *the best place* or *the greatest place*. Everything is over-the-top."

"That's because there are a lot of great places in New York," Dalton said. "I'm not putting down your beloved Wisconsin, but

I'm willing to bet that gastronomically we have you bested. By a lot."

She put her hands on her hips and gave him a withering stare. "Sure, just make fun of my home state. You're not even a New Yorker. You're from Connecticut."

"True enough." He grinned and took a sip from his champagne flute. "I'm a wannabe New Yorker."

"I saw right through you," she said and laughed.

Brenna wandered over to the piano and began playing softly, her fingers plinking out a tune Callie didn't recognize. Deborah leaned in to say, "She's very accomplished on the violin, but she just started taking piano lessons."

Before Callie could answer, Cece floated into the room, wearing an ivory-colored cocktail dress. "I'm sorry for being late," she said, approaching the group. Close up, she looked exactly as she did in the video clips online and yet completely different. More alive, more vibrant. Callie had seen plenty of celebrities in New York, and usually they looked smaller and more ordinary in real life than they did on the screen. With Cece, it was the opposite. Her whispery voice was not whispery anymore. Her posture was more assured, her movements more forthright. Was it that she appeared more confident? Maybe. Callie couldn't name what had changed, but it was undeniable.

Cece went right to Callie and Lauren and gave them each a hug. Somehow she knew exactly who each of them were and spoke as if they were already acquainted. "It's been crazy, as I'm sure you know," she said, gesturing toward Brenna at the piano. "We are so protective of Brenna that for her to even leave the building alone is unheard of." She leaned in and said to Callie, "When we realized she was missing, I felt sick. I have never been so afraid in my life. Having her back is the best gift I've ever been given. If you ever need anything—a favor, a job, a recommendation, anything at all—I'm here for you. I really mean it. I am in your debt."

Callie felt the press of her hand on her arm and found herself smiling. "It was nothing, really. We were glad to help."

Lauren looked around and said, "Is this being filmed?"

"Filmed?" Cece's nose wrinkled questioningly.

"For one of your online videos?"

"Oh, no," she said with a wave of her hand. "I'm taking a break from that for the time being. I'm regrouping and going in a new direction."

"Really? How exciting." Callie took a sip of her champagne.

Cece nodded. "It is exciting. I can't say too much about it just yet, because the details are still being worked out, but I know I'll have less of a public profile and will be doing more work behind the scenes."

"I'll miss seeing your videos," Callie said. "But I certainly understand wanting to do something different."

"That's it exactly," Cece said. "I was due for a change."

Callie reflected on how ordinary this seemed—people standing and talking politely. Somehow she'd expected to feel a little intimidated. The Vanderhavens' home was a bit much, ostentatious some might call it, but the family itself wasn't that different from Callie's own family. Based on the little she knew of Deborah Vanderhaven, she'd expected her to put on airs, but that wasn't the case at all. In person, she was just a mother and wife. Better dressed than the average citizen, but not snobby in the least.

The realization allowed Callie to relax. She listened as Lauren and Greta talked about Greta's upbringing in Wisconsin. Watching them converse, she thought, *This is nice.*

For the next two hours, the Vanderhavens feted Callie and Lauren. They drank champagne and ate delicacies until they were full. Brenna played two songs on her violin, after which she bowed and they all applauded. Afterward, they were given a tour of the apartment, with Cece making a point to show them where their favorite clips had been filmed.

When they returned to the living room, Mr. Vanderhaven asked everyone to be seated while he stood facing them. "If you will indulge me, I'd like to say a few words." Everyone settled into their seats and looked at him expectantly. When the room was completely quiet, he said, "They say you never know what you have until it's lost, and now I know that this is true. I have been a creature of habit, a man who has defined myself by my successes in business. I have always felt that the measure of my worth is what I've accomplished, and by that I mean what I have accomplished in a quantifiable way. I have a competitive streak as well, something I've always prided myself on."

He met Callie's eyes, and she saw the glint of a tear in his eye. He cleared his throat and continued. "It wasn't until I thought that something unthinkable had happened to my daughter, that maybe we'd lost her forever, that I was able to look back at my entire life with laser-sharp focus and could see the depth of my miscalculation. Everything I'd worked so hard to accumulate meant nothing. None of my money or connections made a bit of difference when it came to bringing my daughter back. Ultimately, it was only through the kindness of strangers that her safety was ensured."

Callie felt like she had to say something, so she murmured, "We were happy to help." She'd had enough champagne to feel warm and caring toward everyone in the room.

Harry said, "While my daughter was missing, I made a promise to God that I would be a new man if she was restored to us, and I want to say here and now, in front of my family and our guests, that I intend to make good on my promise. You may have noticed that I'm now home for dinner every evening?" He directed this to Brenna, who bobbed her head, smiling. "There will be other changes as well. We're going to start taking family vacations. I'm not going to miss any more school events or holidays. I know I failed you, Cece, and I apologize for that, but from now on you have my word—I will be a better man."

Cece got up and threw her arms around her father's neck. "You didn't fail me, Dad. I always understood that you had to work."

"I didn't *have* to work as much as I did," he said apologetically. "I was driven and didn't have my priorities straight. I have so many regrets."

The awkward silence that followed was broken by Dalton, who stood and raised his glass. "Let's make a toast—to the importance of family!"

"To family!"

"I'll drink to that," Roger said, and there was the clinking of glasses all around.

"Oh!" Cece said after they all took a sip. "I almost forgot." She held up one finger. "Just give me a minute. I'll be right back." She disappeared from the room, and when she returned a minute later, she had a wrapped gift in her hands. Behind her followed a woman in black pants and a button-down shirt carrying an even bigger wrapped present. Silently the woman set the gift on the floor next to where Mrs. Vanderhaven sat.

Cece handed the smaller present to Callie. "Just a little something to say thank you for returning Brenna to us."

"Thank you."

"Open it!" Brenna said.

All eyes were on Callie as she tore open the paper, revealing a plain box not much bigger than a shoebox. She lifted the lid. Inside were two smaller boxes—one was a jewelry box holding a Tiffany necklace, the other a gift card for an upscale new restaurant. Callie said, "This is so nice, but it's really not necessary."

"We wanted to do it," Cece said firmly. "It's our pleasure, truly."

Harry said, "When you and your husband go out to dinner, think kindly of us and remember that you saved our little girl."

Callie said, "Thank you. We certainly will."

"And now for Lauren," Cece said, getting the larger package and handing it to Lauren.

"But I didn't do anything," Lauren said. "Honestly, this isn't necessary."

"Oh, but we wanted to," Cece said. "Brenna and I had so much fun shopping for your gift. I think you're going to love it."

Brenna leaned over excitedly. "You're going to *really* love it."

Lauren and Callie exchanged puzzled glances, and then Lauren said, "Thank you." The words came out almost as a question, a sentiment Callie shared. She'd only let the Vanderhavens know recently that Lauren would be coming this evening instead of Colton. They'd never met her, so how would they know to shop for a gift she'd love?

Lauren untied the bow and set the ribbon on the end table next to her, then lifted the lid. She gasped, her mouth open wide, and the blood left her face. From where Callie sat, the contents of the box weren't visible. She craned her neck but still couldn't see. "What is it?" she asked impatiently.

Slowly, Lauren lifted a baby girl's dress, a veritable cloud of soft lavender ruffles, held it up for a second, and then lowered it back into the box.

"There's more too," Brenna said, jumping out of her seat. "There's a silver rattle and a stuffed giraffe. The giraffe is so cute. When you squeeze it, it squeaks." She got up and went next to Lauren, then reached into the box to hold up the giraffe so everyone in the room could see.

"Brenna picked out the giraffe," Cece said. "The rattle is a keepsake. After she's born, you can get it engraved with her name and birthdate. There's a certificate that comes with it that covers the engraving."

"Do you have a name picked out yet?" This from Deborah, who smiled brightly. "That's the fun part. I knew I would have a Cecelia from the time I was a junior in high school."

"My dad picked out my name," Brenna said, still holding the giraffe.

"Yes, I did." Harry smiled at his younger daughter.

Callie watched all this, wondering where the Vanderhavens had gotten the impression that Lauren was having a baby. She waited for her sister to correct them, but Lauren just sat there, stunned.

"Do you like it?" Brenna said.

When Lauren finally spoke, her voice cracked with emotion. "I love it," she said. "How did you know? I haven't told anyone . . ."

"Summer told me," Brenna said. "She said she was getting a new cousin. We saw you out the window, and she said you were her aunt Lauren and you were having a baby girl."

"Summer told you this?" Lauren sounded awestruck.

"Uh-huh." Brenna nodded in confirmation. "She said you were going to have the cutest baby girl. She said you should name her Winter 'cause that's when your baby is going to be born. In the wintertime. Summer thought that was so funny."

Lauren gulped, her throat pulsing.

"Lauren?" Callie asked. "Is this true? Are you pregnant?"

The room went quiet. The box slid off Lauren's lap as her eyes shut. Her body wilting, she collapsed sideways in the chair. Harry leaped up. "She's fainted," he said.

In an instant, everyone was up on their feet, helping to hold Lauren in place so she didn't slide out of the chair onto the floor. "I'll call 911," Roger said, getting his phone out of his pocket.

"No, wait!" Callie said. "Her eyes are open now." She laid a hand on her sister's forehead. "Lauren, are you okay?"

Lauren blinked. "I'm so sorry. I'm not sure what happened."

"I fainted twice when I was pregnant with Cece," Deborah said. "Both times I was just overly hungry. Make sure you tell your doctor, though, just to be on the safe side."

"I think I'm okay," she said, sitting up. "I just got lightheaded for a minute there."

Lauren's faint brought an end to the evening. The Vanderhavens insisted on having their driver take the sisters home. After saying their goodbyes and exchanging hugs, Harry Vanderhaven, carrying their gifts, accompanied them into the elevator, through the lobby, and out the front door where the car, a long black sedan, awaited. He gave the gifts to the driver, then opened the door for the women. As Lauren slid inside, Callie said, "Thank you for a lovely evening."

Harry smiled. "The pleasure was ours."

As the car pulled away, she glanced back to see him still standing on the sidewalk, his arm raised in a final goodbye wave. Turning to Lauren, she patted her arm. "You okay?"

"Physically I'm fine." Lauren shook her head in wonder. "Emotionally, though, I'm still sort of reeling." She took in a deep breath. "She talked to Summer, and Summer told her I was having a baby girl. How can that be?"

"I know," Callie said sympathetically. "It's a lot to take in."

Her sister nodded. "That's for sure."

"Once you come to accept it, though, it's really kind of wonderful. At least that's how it's been for me."

CHAPTER 35

 *wo years later*

TWO YEARS after Greta met Dalton in Times Square, he suggested they go out for a night on the town, their town—New York City. He'd gotten tickets to a Broadway show and made reservations at her favorite restaurant, Gallagher's Steakhouse on West Fifty-Second Street. Prior to that night, they'd discussed their future and agreed that neither one could imagine their world without the other one in it. The prospect of marriage had come up as well. They both saw it on the horizon but hadn't discussed a timeline.

That night, Greta was fairly certain he was going to propose, and so she dressed in one of Cece's newest designer dresses and wore a pair of heels higher than her usual. Cece fussed over her appearance, trying different variations of hair and jewelry until they were satisfied with the final choices. "Hair down. Drop earrings," Cece declared, brushing her hands together. "It's the best combination for you, Greta. You look gorgeous."

When they heard a knock on the door, Greta was still putting the finishing touches on her makeup, so Cece said, "Don't rush. I'll get it. He can wait a few minutes."

Greta brushed her cheeks with a wide angled brush, took a step back from the mirror and smiled, and then took a tissue and lightly wiped off some of the bronzer. Even allowing for the evening light, it seemed a bit much. She heard Dalton's voice as Cece let him in, and what sounded like a friendly conversation. A few minutes later, Cece pushed open the bathroom door and grinned, saying, "Your date is here, and guess what? Turns out it's James Bond."

Seeing him in his impeccably tailored suit, Greta saw the resemblance. Dalton looked like a younger, sexier James Bond. The man did clean up well. He whistled as she walked into the room. "Cece is right. You do look gorgeous."

Greta felt herself blush. "She's my cousin and my stylist. She *has* to say that."

"Well, I am neither, and I speak the truth. You look exceptionally beautiful, Greta."

Gathering up her bag, Greta gave Cece one last hug before they headed out.

"Don't wait up," Dalton said as he pulled the door shut behind him.

Standing in the hallway, hand in hand, they were surprised when the elevator doors opened to reveal Brenna and Nanny, Brenna holding the leash of her dog, Rusty. Brenna's eyes got wide at the sight of them. "You look really pretty, Greta."

"Thank you."

"Told you." Dalton nudged her with a wink.

"Both of you look wonderful," Nanny said, then grabbed the leash to keep Rusty from jumping on them. Rusty was a rescue, just like the Griffins' dog, Baxter. He was a mixed breed, copper-colored, and he definitely had some miniature poodle in the mix. After Brenna had picked him out at the shelter, her father had declared him "one rusty little troublemaker." The name stuck. At seven months, he was still very much in puppy mode and needed constant attention, but Brenna had promised her father she'd take care of him, and she'd been true to her word. She and Nanny attended dog training classes in their home and followed through with everything the instructor told them. Greta was impressed with how Brenna had taken complete responsibility for her new pet. It was astounding, too, how the dog already seemed partial to Brenna, following her around the apartment and responding to her voice. It was as if they were made for each other.

Now Brenna said, "Where are you going?"

Dalton leaned over to give Rusty a rub behind the ears. "Out to see a play and then to dinner."

"It sounds lovely," Nanny said.

They parted ways outside the building, with Nanny and Brenna heading down the sidewalk toward the park and Dalton and Greta waiting for their ride to the show.

At the theater, Greta surreptitiously looked to see if he had a box tucked in his suit jacket pocket, but there was nothing to suggest he was packing a diamond ring.

Afterward they walked from the theater to the restaurant. Upon greeting them, the host said to Greta, in a charming Irish accent, "Why, don't you look beautiful this evening, miss," making her blush.

Not to be outdone, Dalton said, "She *always* looks beautiful." After they were seated at the white-linen-covered table, he said, "I can't believe the nerve of that guy, flirting with my date right in front of me."

Greta grinned. "I think that's just his usual shtick."

"He can put his shtick elsewhere."

They drank wine and laughed and talked, one of those rare evenings that wasn't quite as rare now that she was dating Dalton Bishop. After eating one of the most delicious meals of her life, she waited for the moment when Dalton would leave his chair and get down on one knee, proposing before God and all the other diners at the restaurant. She even left to use the restroom to give him some time to prepare. But the moment never came. When they were finished, Dalton paid the bill, leaving a generous tip to reward excellent service, and they walked out into the night air.

"Now what?" Greta said.

Dalton took her hand and looked upward. "Will you look at that? I do believe there's a full moon tonight."

She tipped her chin up. "I don't see the moon." Presumably it was obscured by one of the buildings.

"Trust me, it's there. Work with me here, Greta." He had a grin in his voice. "You know," he said, his voice becoming theatrical, "the most beautiful night sky I ever saw was on the Bow Bridge during a full moon."

She'd heard him say these words before, shortly after they'd met, and now she had an idea of how this was going to go. Realizing that this was really going to happen, Greta felt a rush of emotion—pure love mixed with excitement and anticipation. "I think I remember something about that."

A sleek black horse pulling a white carriage approached, the clip-clop of hooves slowing until it stopped directly in front of them. Dalton lifted a hand to signal the driver. The horse threw back his head and nickered.

The driver leaned over the side of his seat. "Mr. Bishop and Miss Hansen?"

"Yes," Dalton said. "That would be us." He helped Greta up into the carriage and then hopped up himself, and they were off, the horse trotting slowly toward Central Park.

Greta said, "Funny how he pulled up at the exact second we walked out."

"I texted him when you were in the bathroom."

The enormity of the occasion was clear to her, and because

of this she wanted to remember every detail—the cool feel of the night air, the other vehicles that wove around them, the sidewalks filled with pedestrians coming and going from Broadway shows. Greta was enraptured by all of it, especially basking in Dalton's smile and the feeling of his arm around her shoulder and the thought of all the trouble he'd gone to in order to orchestrate this evening. As much as she already loved him, she felt that now she loved him even more. It was happening as if in a dream or a movie. Surreal. She felt as if she were part of it and observing it at the same time.

It would be funny if he didn't propose after all of this. Well, then, she'd just have to do it herself.

The carriage couldn't take them all the way to the bridge, but the driver went as far as he could and said he'd wait. As Greta and Dalton walked down the path, she noticed that he'd mysteriously acquired a bouquet of roses, tied with ribbons. Walking into the clearing just before the bridge, Dalton stopped and looked up. "Now do you see the moon?"

It would be hard to miss, hanging as it was, a bright gold orb seemingly just for them. She nodded. "Now I see it. Good planning, Mr. Bishop."

"I arranged it just for you."

Now he was pulling her by the hand, an impatience in his step that made her laugh. They weren't alone on the bridge, other people were coming and going, but she only had eyes for Dalton. When they got to the middle of the bridge, he slowed to a stop and faced her, his expression solemn. "Greta, after I met you, I realized what people mean when they say *falling in love*. From the start, I fell for you in a big way, and every day I fall in love with you all over again. I can't imagine not having you in my life." He paused and took a deep breath, then reached into the middle of the bouquet and pulled out a ring box. Still holding the flowers, he dropped to one knee and flipped open the box. "Greta Hansen, will you marry me?"

She leaned down to his level, cupped his face in her hands, and with a trembling heart said, "Yes, I will." He lifted his face to hers, and their lips met in a kiss. He stood up and put the ring on her finger, and she choked back tears. It was everything she'd hoped for and yet so much better.

Behind them she heard one person clapping slowly and loudly. Soon others joined in, and there was whooping and a man yelling, "Congratulations!" Complete strangers who'd witnessed the biggest moment of her life. She smiled their way, bowed slightly, and said, "Thank you."

Two middle-aged women came up and asked to see the ring. Greta held her hand out, and they admired it. The taller of the two told Dalton, "You did good. It's gorgeous."

As they walked away, a young woman, her boyfriend trailing behind her, approached and said, "As soon as he got down on one knee, I got out my phone and started filming." She held the phone out for them to watch, and again, Greta felt as if she was living someone else's life. When it was finished, the woman got Dalton's number and texted him the clip right away.

As they walked back to the carriage, Greta held on to his arm and said, "This was a perfect night."

"I'm glad. I thought you might think it lacked creativity. It's kind of textbook rom-com." He pointed upward. "The bridge, the moon. Getting down on one knee. Even those random people clapping. Some might say it's kind of cheesy."

"As it turns out," she said, "I'm a huge fan of cheesy."

CHAPTER 36

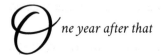 *ne year after that*

BRENNA'S MOTHER had said it was a perfect day for a June wedding: sunny and warm, not a cloud in the sky. Everyone in the wedding party had arrived at the church on time and were now getting ready in their respective rooms. Even though the groomsmen were on the opposite side of the building, down a long hall past the bathrooms, their raucous laughter could be heard all the way into the room where the women were getting their makeup done and hair styled. Brenna got the impression that the guys were having a lot more fun than the bride and bridesmaids.

"What could possibly be so funny?" Greta asked, twisting around as far as she could, given that the stylist had a section of her hair wrapped around the barrel of a curling iron. A wrinkle furrowed her forehead. Brenna had wondered the same thing. There was an air of nervousness and anticipation in the women's room that apparently was lacking in the men's.

Cece, who was getting her makeup done, paused to say, "Brenna, why don't you go spy on them and see what they're doing?"

Brenna jumped out of her chair, eager to go. She'd been the first in the stylist's chair, and they were finished with her. Since she was only eleven, they'd kept the makeup light and her hair simple, just a few loose waves falling over her shoulders.

The third bridesmaid, Jacey, Greta's friend from back home, grinned. "Good idea. Go listen and report back to us."

Brenna didn't need any further urging. She left the room and went down the hallway, following the sounds of male camaraderie. Her mother along with Dalton's mother and Greta's mom were in the church proper, checking on the floral arrangements and making small talk. No one noticed as she walked past.

When she got to the groomsmen's closed door, she stood outside listening, trying to differentiate who was speaking, but it was difficult. She knew Dalton's voice, but she'd only just met his friend Will and Dalton's brother, Grant, at the rehearsal the day before. Greta's brother, Travis, was related to her and looked slightly familiar, but he was nearly a stranger as well. She pressed her ear against the door, trying to make out what they were talking about, but there didn't seem to be an actual conversation taking place. Their voices were a tangle, a knot of laughter and exclamations.

"Dude, stop it!"

"Bro, that is the worst bow tie I've ever seen!"

"Cut me some slack, will you? This isn't something I do much."

Inside she heard a scuffle, like boys roughhousing, but these were grown men. Could they really be goofing around right before a wedding?

"Ow! Let go!"

She raised her hand and rapped on the door, and the sounds

stopped. A few seconds later, the door opened and Dalton's face appeared in the gap. "Hey, Brenna!" he said, a smile spreading across his face. That was something she really liked about him. He always seemed happy to see her and never talked down to her. "Is everything okay?"

"Everything's okay," she said. "We were just wondering . . . what's so funny?" She realized as she spoke that she was supposed to be spying on them, which presumably meant not giving too much away, but it was too late to take it back.

Dalton grinned. "Nothing earthshaking," he said. "Just a bunch of idiots who aren't used to getting dressed so formally. We're having a bit of a bow tie crisis here."

"Oh," she said, smoothing down the front of her dress. The fabric, a silvery blue, floated as she walked. Cece had designed Greta's gown and the bridesmaids' dresses. Designing bridal attire had become Cece's specialty in the last few years, and now she was custom designing wedding dresses for the women her mother called "everyone who is anyone." Brenna found this somewhat confusing, because wasn't everyone also anyone? No matter how hard she tried she couldn't figure it out, but she also didn't dwell on it. Today she was one of those wearing Cece's coveted designs, and she understood the allure. When she looked in the mirror, she saw a special, more dressed-up version of herself.

"You look really pretty," Dalton said, as if reading her mind. Before she could respond, he said, "Can you do me a favor?"

"Sure."

"If I wrote a note to Greta, would you deliver it to her?"

"Yes."

"Wait just a minute." The door closed, and she heard the men's voices again, more subdued this time. When Dalton returned, he had a piece of paper folded into a small square. On the outside he'd written Greta's name. "Don't show this to anyone but Greta, okay?"

She nodded.

"Promise?"

"I promise."

"Don't read it," he said, a warning tone in his voice.

"I won't."

Back in the bride's room, Brenna wordlessly handed the note to Greta, who took it and began to unfold it.

"So?" Cece asked. "What's going on?"

"They're having trouble with their bow ties," Brenna said.

"Oh, is that all?" Cece sounded disappointed.

She shot a glance at Greta, who was silently reading, a smile lighting up her face.

"What's that?" Jacey asked.

"A note from Dalton," Greta said, her eyes still on the page.

"What does it say?"

"It says he loves me."

Brenna could tell from the look in her eyes that there was more to it than that, but no one pressed the issue.

As the stylists finished their work, they heard the sounds of the guests arriving. By then the mothers had stopped by to assure them they all looked beautiful.

And then, before Brenna knew it, they were lined up outside the doors and the music had begun. As the youngest and short-est, she was the first to walk down the aisle, something that had been fine during rehearsal but was nerve-racking in a church filled with people. To get through it, she concentrated on walking at just the right pace and staring ahead at Dalton and the groomsmen, who were already lined up in front. Dalton gave her an encouraging smile, and as she smiled right back, she felt the tension leave her shoulders. When she reached her place, she stopped and turned, relieved to be finished.

Despite the fact that this was Dalton and Greta's wedding, she found she knew quite a few people attending. Nanny was there, of course, right in the second row. Cece's friends, Katrina and Vance had flown in from California for the event. Lauren and Callie were there as well, along with their husbands. They had left their children at home. Lauren's baby was now an adorable two-year-old. They'd named her Brenna and had given her the middle name Winter, something that had delighted Brenna when she found out. Brenna hadn't seen them in person since the one evening when they'd come to her house. Still, Greta had wanted to invite them. They had declined attending the reception, but they said they wouldn't miss the wedding ceremony, which was, as Greta said, the most important part anyway.

For Brenna, the best part of being the first to walk down the aisle, aside from getting it over with, was being able to view the rest of the bridal party as they walked in. Brenna watched as first Jacey and then Cece came up to join her. Once they were standing alongside her, the music changed, the organist playing Mendelssohn's "Wedding March," and Greta appeared on the arm of her father. Everyone in the church rose to their feet, guests murmuring admiring comments as she approached.

Greta looked, Brenna decided, splendiferous. It was a vocabulary word she'd been introduced to at school but never had reason to use. Greta's dress was stunning, of course, and her hair gorgeous, but that wasn't what made her look so outstandingly beautiful. It was the look on her face. She absolutely beamed with happiness, matching Dalton's expression.

Everyone in the church noticed it. They couldn't help but see it. Brenna's own parents looked delighted to be there, her father smiling down on her mom as if reliving the joy of their own wedding day. Her father had kept his word since Brenna had been found, and their lives had changed dramatically since then. Family dinners. Family vacations. He'd begun to help her with homework. She once even saw him load up the dishwasher.

More recently, he'd turned down a big meeting in London to attend this wedding. Doing so meant missing out on some kind of big deal that instead went to a competitor. Brenna had overheard the speakerphone conversation the day he'd told them his decision. After some persuasive arguments, the man on the other end of the line gave up, saying, "Sounds like you don't value doing business with me."

"I do value your business," her dad had said. "But I value my family more than anything."

More than anything. That's how much he loved them.

* * *

A YEAR OF WEDDING PLANNING, and it all came down to this moment, to the two of them standing in a church in front of God and their loved ones, with her vowing to love, honor, and cherish Dalton all the days of her life.

They'd talked about writing their vows, but the idea of having to say them in front of a large crowd made Greta nervous, so instead they'd decided to rely on the traditional ones. "They've been good enough for other people for centuries; I think they'll work for us," Dalton had said.

Now they stood together while the minister asked Greta if she took Dalton as her lawfully wedded husband. She heard everything he said, the words *sickness and health* floating over her as she looked into Dalton's eyes. She would be making a promise for all the days of her life, and she was so ready to do it. Thank goodness she'd opted not to write her own vows. Memorizing the words would have been stressful, and she would have been too emotional to read off a sheet of paper. As it was, she was relieved only to have to remember two words.

"I do."

The minister turned to Dalton and said, "And do you, Dalton, promise to take Greta as your lawfully wedded wife, to have and to hold, in sickness and health, all the days of your life?"

When he said "I do" and smiled at her, eyes shining with excitement, she felt like her heart might burst with joy.

A simple promise from each of them with an infinite number of implications. They had no way of knowing what the future would hold for either of them, but with love, faith, and hope on their side, they would get through it together.

The ceremony, the one she'd anticipated for so long, went by in a beautiful, surreal blur. After she heard the words "I now pronounce you husband and wife," Dalton swept her into his arms and planted a kiss even before the minister added, "You may kiss the bride."

The guests laughed at his eagerness, but it didn't surprise her. The note he'd had Brenna deliver had said, "Greta, I love you so much, and I can't wait for our first kiss as husband and wife."

ACKNOWLEDGMENTS

This time around, Kay Ehlers and Michelle San Juan volunteered to be my early readers. (Or maybe they were drafted?) Regardless, many thanks to both of them for their thoughtful comments and excellent catches. I appreciate their help and never take it for granted.

Copyeditor Jessica Fogleman served as both my editor and teacher. I've learned so much from her over the years and was overjoyed to have a chance to work with her again. I will gladly claim any remaining errors as mine since I was the source of the trouble to begin with.

Once again, I want to thank my family for their love and support. Greg, Charlie, Rachel, Maria, and Jack—I love you all.

To the My Book Tribe Facebook group: you've added so much to my life, both personally and professionally. I'm raising a glass in your general direction and sending you my fondest appreciation. (If you're reading this and don't belong to My Book Tribe, come on over and join the fun! You aren't going to find a nicer group of readers and authors. https://www.facebook.com/groups/MyBookTribe/)

And finally, a shout-out to my readers. You are the reason I write novels. Your support and reviews keep me going, and I hope to never let you down. From the bottom of my heart, thank you.